indefinite

BOOK ONE IN THE INDEFINITE DUET

the salvation series

NEW YORK TIMES AND *USA TODAY* BESTSELLING AUTHOR

CORINNE MICHAELS

Cover Design:
Sarah Hansen, Okay Creations

Editing:
Ashley Williams, AW Editing

Proofreading:
Michele Ficht
Janice Owen

Interior Design:
Stacey Blake, Champagne Book Design

Cover photo © Perrywinkle Photography

indefinite

dedication

To my 9 girls.
May everyone in this world know a friendship like ours.

chapter one

QUINN

"WHAT DO YOU WANT FROM ME?" I ASK ASHTON AS SHE'S tossing her clothes into her bag. "Apparently, I can't figure out what it is! I'm trying, but it still is not good enough! Don't you see that?"

"Trying? How are you trying?"

We stand in my bedroom, back at square one. "I'm not doing a full four years—just the one!"

My team is deploying, and they're down a few bodies. I can't be the asshole who decides that now is the time to turn in my gear. I know that was the plan, but things change. Plus, I'm not ready to walk away. I need to be there, need to command and lead my team. There aren't many snipers with my experience, and I can't handle the thought of someone dying because I'm not there.

Her anger is palpable as she uses more force than necessary to pack. "And then what? After that, what excuse will it be then?"

"I don't know."

I don't even bother trying to lie because there *will* be another one. The truth is that being a SEAL is who I am. I'm not ready to hang up my boots.

"Right. Because you're not going to walk away, and you're not going to keep your promises to me. Because it's not about us or me. It's about you and your career."

I groan and start to pace. "What would you rather me do? Let the team be vulnerable?"

She shakes her head. "That isn't the point, Quinn. It's that you have had me in this waiting game for years! *Years* of you saying that once you were out of the navy, we'd start a family. We'd have everything. You were the one who put this on a time-line, not me." Ashton takes a few steps closer. "I would've married you two years ago and been pregnant already, but you said you wanted to wait."

Here we go. Right back to how I'm the one who's wasting her time, and maybe I am, but I'm sick and tired of it all falling on me. "I always let you down, right? I'm the bad guy because I didn't want to start a life when, at any moment, you could deal with the knock on the door. God for-fucking-bid I protect you from that level of pain. I'm the reason, right? Not that you can't understand why I'm not ready to give it up or that I will *never* get married while I'm active. I've seen that side, and it'll destroy us."

She turns, laughs once, and then goes back to packing. "I knew this would happen. I trust you, let you back in, and think that things are finally going to change, only to be reminded that it's not possible! You act like you're protecting me, but we both know that's a lie. It's you! You are who you're protecting! Not me. And don't worry about the destruction, Quinn, the navy didn't have a hand in that."

I'm tired. I'm so fucking tired of this. I've done just about everything she's asked except put a ring on her finger. Why? Because I'm not good enough for her. I will never be. She is smart, funny, drop-dead gorgeous, and everything I've ever wanted, but I can't give her what she wants. I've been living on borrowed time with her from the moment we met.

Looking at her in front me, knowing she's so close but her heart is already a million miles away, breaks something inside me.

I may not be worthy of her, but I damn sure want to keep her.

How selfish am I?

"If you think that, then this is why we always fall apart . . ." I nearly choke on the words as I wrap my arms around her because I can't stop myself. I have to touch her. "If you believe that," I say in a whisper, "then you don't know me at all. I'm giving you what you want by walking away. You want a family, and I can't do that while my family is my team."

My heart is beating hard against my chest walls as her body starts to tremble. This is what we do. We fight, we make each other crazy, we push each other away, and then we crash back together.

Like a never-ending war that we keep fighting because we can't stop. She and I will always be on opposite sides, unable to create a treaty.

"Can't or won't?" she asks.

"Does it matter?"

She wants to be my world. She wants me not to reenlist, move to New York, and marry her like I promised I would. It just is not who I am. I thought I could, but then those papers were in front of me and I saw the guys. If I got out next week, it would be the biggest mistake I made, bigger than even letting her walk away from me. I am a navy SEAL. I'm a frogman. I'm a goddamn warrior, and I can't give that up.

"I guess it doesn't." Her voice splinters and so does my heart. After a few seconds, she sniffs as her shoulders fall. "It could be so simple for us."

I bury my face in her dark red hair and brush my nose against the back of her neck. "I can't do it. I can't give up this life." In her heart, I think she knows this. "Not even for you, *fragolina*."

I hope that the term of endearment softens her, makes her see. She hates that I call her little strawberry, but that's what she is. She's fire on the outside and sweet in the center. She tries to guard herself, tries not to bruise or break, but she's delicate.

"So, that's it? You're going to extend due to this deployment and then reenlist? No matter what? Regardless of the fact that you told me you wouldn't? That I've been waiting for this so we could start our life?"

"I'm signing the papers for an extension when we get overseas. I don't know if I'll reenlist or ride out the deployment. I just need time, Ashton."

I won't lie to her about this. I lie about other things—like how I feel about her or what I want . . . really want in my heart—but I won't make her think there's a life I can offer her that I can't give.

"I love you, Quinn. Against my better judgment, I love you, and you will never love me back." Ashton's quiet sobs break me apart. "I can't keep going like this. You promised me that the last deployment was it and then we'd start a family together. I can't spend the rest of my life hoping you'll see that I'm right in front of you, waiting for you to share your heart with me, waiting for you to choose me."

I love her more than she can ever know. I just can't tell her. I have to protect her from loving a man like me. My heart isn't mine to give—it belongs to my teammates. I fight against emotion because not having anything to lose makes the idea of dying easier to handle.

I've lost too many men on missions. Held too many widows as they stood in front of that flag-covered casket.

Loving Ashton gives me something to come home for, and that makes me weak. I can't be that when I'm gone. I have to be smart and keep my head in the game so I can make sure everyone is safe.

I hold her close, needing to feel her body against mine for just a while longer. Each second that passes is one I'll keep forever. Her head rests against my chest. "You shouldn't love me," I say against her neck, closing my eyes and breathing her in. "You shouldn't because I don't deserve it."

"I know. Yet, here I am, waiting for you to say the words that will cause me to walk out that door like you always do."

And here is where I fail her. Time and time again. I delude myself into thinking that, if I can keep her at arm's length while still giving her what she needs, we can find a way through our issues, but we can't. Ashton doesn't love in half measures, and she sure as fuck doesn't deserve that from me.

However, hurting her on purpose feels like torture. "I can't say them this time." I inhale her floral scent, committing it to memory because I'm sure this will be the last time I see her.

It has to end here, but that doesn't mean I can't steal a little of the fire and life she's brimming with.

"Tell me that you'll come back," she pleads. "Tell me you'll come home and that we can finally have this life together. If you can give me that, I'll wait for you."

I leave tomorrow for seven months, and I don't know if I can walk away from this life. "That's a promise I can't make." Her hand's lift, wiping away a tear, and that's my breaking point. I release her. "You should go back to New York."

When Ashton turns, her blue eyes are filled with unshed tears and a mixture of love and hate. Her lips tremble as she struggles for control of her emotions. I'm completely stoic. I won't let her see my hurt. I won't give her the one thing she wants and needs from me. If I'm going to give her up, it'll be so much easier if she hates me.

When she thinks of me, she'll remember anger and bitter disappointment. She'll only see the version of me standing in front of her right now, the one who couldn't give a shit less about her feelings. That man is easier to walk away from and move on.

"Tell me, Quinn, say you don't love me."

"I don't love you," I lie.

I'm dying. My heart is being ripped from my chest. This is the worst kind of pain. It's deep in my bones, shattering each one in slow snaps because I know it's going to cause her pain.

"You're lying."

She knows me better than I've tried to allow.

"No, I'm not. I don't love you, Ashton. I don't love anyone or anything other than this life. You should go."

Her hand rests on my chest, right over my heart. "You can lie to me all you want . . ." She pauses, eyes locked on mine. "But you can't lie to yourself. You may not want to love me, but you do. The saddest part of all of this is that, when you realize it . . . when you're home from this deployment and all the guys are hugging their wives and kids, it'll be too late. I'll be gone. Maybe I'll be with someone else. Maybe I'll be happy with someone else, living the life you promised me, but no matter what I'm doing, it'll be without you." Ashton leans forward, pressing her lips to mine.

In my head, I'm screaming, beating the shit out of myself to wake up and stop her. Everything wants to fight for her, tell her she's right and I love her. Marry her today. Give her the kids, family, and life she wants.

It's all right there.

I could have it.

I could have her, but I'm a coward.

She waits for a beat, watching to see if I'll say something, but I know that we'll be back here again. So I don't move.

Her eyes close and then she turns, grabs her bag, and walks to the door.

This is the last chance. I clench my fists so tight I'm sure I'll draw blood.

"Goodbye, Quinn. I hope it all works out for you."

The door shuts as Ashton walks away. I never understood the term *heartbreak* until now. Too many emotions flood me at one time, and I start to go after her, but when I get to the front door, I can't do it. I slam my fist into the solid wood and welcome the physical pain because it's nothing compared to what is going on inside me.

Fuck love.

Fuck this.

Fuck it all.

Now I'm ready to deploy.

chapter two

ASHTON

~ *Six Months Later* ~

"I'M GOING TO HAVE A BABY," I TELL CATHERINE AS WE SIT on the beach by her apartment.

"I'm sorry, you're *what*?"

"A baby. I'm going to get me one."

She looks at me with confusion and a little bit of fear. "So, you're pregnant? I didn't even know you were dating someone."

I laugh. "No, I'm not pregnant . . . yet. Since I walked away from Quinn, I've become a damn nun. I tried to date that one guy, and I spent all night thinking about how he was too thin and couldn't protect me from a fly. Then all I did was measure the rest of his body against the chicken shit."

Quinn is not small—anywhere. He's wide, tall, has muscles that have muscles, and I could talk shit to anyone and he'd be able to kick their ass. At least, that was the feeling I had around him. I loved to test that theory too, which usually proved to be correct, but he didn't think it was as funny as I did. Also, it was his arms. His arms were so big and strong that I would hold on to them, loving that my fingers couldn't come close to touching because of how thick they were. I really miss them.

Catherine sighs. "Okay, well, I'm missing where the baby part comes in. Usually, there's a man involved when creating the baby."

I look at her round belly, both happy for her and jealous of her. She has it all. She has Jackson, her company, *and* a bun in the oven. It's everything I want. Sure, I put on this tough-girl exterior and pretend that I don't want or need a man. While that is somewhat true, if it were the actual case, I never would've fallen for Quinn. I wouldn't have spent the last six months agonizing over whether I was a fool for walking away from him.

And even now, after months of zero contact, I miss the stupid bastard.

I sit around, wondering how he is. I write emails I'll never send. I call my friend Natalie to get updates about him through Liam, who is deployed with him. She's dealing with raising two kids, her husband being gone, and my crazy ass who won't hit send.

"I'm tired of waiting. I'm getting old, you're having a kid, and Gretchen will probably have one after her wedding. Everyone is living, and I'm stagnant."

"Or stuck on repeat."

I glare at her. "There will be no repeat this time."

Quinn and I are not getting back together. When I walked out that door, I walked out of his life. For good.

There was no misunderstanding regarding our current situation. I asked him to love me, he refused and let me go.

Now I'm going to fly.

"Still, you're going to have to clue me in here."

"I'm an embryologist. I make babies for a living, so, I'm going to do it for myself."

She sits up, crosses her legs, and releases a deep sigh. Here we go. "Ash, are you sure? You want to be a single mother?

Really? You work insane hours. You moved to Brooklyn, which is farther from your parents than you've ever lived before. I also know you want to be married when you start a family."

"Yeah. I do. I want all of that. I want the marriage, the honeymoon, and the perfect life, but I don't have that, Cat. I don't have the guy, the house, the ring, the life . . . you do. You and Gretchen got the great guys while I got Quinn. All I've ever wanted was a baby, and with all the issues my mom had . . . I can't wait."

Catherine doesn't love Quinn, but she always seems to side with him. It's the strangest thing, and I blame Jackson. Him and his navy SEAL brotherhood crap. I'm well aware of how hard deployments are on the guys, that they are hard on Quinn—there was never any question of that. What about what it's like for me, though? What about the fact that his issues became my issues? What about him pushing and pulling me back and forth like we were playing a game of tug-of-war where I ended in the mud at the end of each round?

"You know why he's this way. You knew it when you started dating him."

"And I hoped to fix him."

She rolls her eyes. "That could be your first problem."

"I loved him enough for both of us."

Catherine falls quiet. "I'm sorry, Ash."

"It's fine. I'm done waiting to start my life and have the things that I want. That was the second disastrous relationship I'd been in, and I'm not ready to love anyone else. So, fuck the man, I'm going to get the baby and be just fine."

Quinn has been the last three years of my life, but before him, there was Antonio. God, I loved him. I thought he was the one. Everything with us was perfect. We fit so well, complemented each other in every way. I was so in love with him I thought I could never have found anything like him again, and then I met his wife.

I still can't think of that without wanting to drive to his house and cut off his balls. I'm hoping she did it for me when she found out. I hate him, but then again, he brought me to Quinn.

Who I remember I also hate.

Catherine takes my hand, bringing me to the present. "If that's what you want, then I support you."

I nod once. "It is."

"You know, we may actually get to live out our plan if you have a boy."

Oh, Lord. "I don't think either of us should plan to marry off our babies before they're born."

She laughs. "Still. It would be funny since I'm having a girl. If you have a boy, then they can grow up and fall in love."

"It would be."

I leave to head back to New York in a day, and it feels weird knowing that I won't be around Cat all the time. She's married to her big bad CEO husband, Jackson. They're building an empire, kicking asses, and she's off saving half of Hollywood from their disasters and rehab issues, so I only see her once or twice a week. It's just . . . not the same without her.

Gretchen has moved to Virginia Beach, is engaged to an insanely hot SEAL named Ben, and works for Cole Security Forces. As does pretty much everyone else we know, and then there's me.

The lone wolf.

No boyfriend. No life. Just my job and the love of my city that I will never leave.

"Ash? What's wrong?"

"Nothing," I shake my head with a smile.

"Liar."

After almost twenty years of friendship, she knows me, I know her, and we both know bullshit when we smell it.

"I hate being so far from you. When you left, I always thought that maybe you'd come back. I knew it was dumb because you weren't going to leave Jackson, but I hoped that he'd bring you back to me. Then I let that go and figured that at least I had Gretchen. Now she's gone. I'm just sort of lost."

She sits straighter. "You are *not* lost. You're the only one out of the three of us who has ever been sure of her direction. Now look at you, you're going to have a baby on your own terms. Seriously, that's insanely brave."

Maybe it is, or maybe it's stupid. I probably am also the last one who should have a kid, even if I think I'd be a good mom. I know I want children, and I was raised in a house where we always had family around. They were loud, intrusive, and irritating, but I wouldn't change any of it.

My cousin, who I used to babysit, is engaged. I can't take it.

I wanted a minimum of four kids, but at this rate, I'll be lucky if I have one.

"I'm not going to get my hopes up that it'll work. I know better than anyone else that some women, no matter what, can't have kids."

"Do you truly think you're going to have issues?"

I shrug. "I don't know, but the issues my mom had were hereditary. She is the poster child for fertility issues."

"You're still young. She was older when she tried for you."

I laugh. "We're lying to ourselves if you think we're young, Cat. I'm the same age she was when she started trying. There were forty-three eggs I lost in the time that I was with jackass number one and jackass number two. Eggs that were probably my best chances."

Catherine laughs. "You've been counting your eggs?"

"I'm looking at reality. Those were good childbearing years, which is why I'm glad I froze some."

"I still don't even understand that one."

She doesn't have to. "It's what I do for a living, and I wanted to know what a woman went through. Then I figured I might as well keep them because I have no idea if I've still got any left."

I'm being slightly dramatic, but there's also truth to it. I'm not twenty-nine anymore. I'm getting older, and if I keep putting it off to meet the "right guy" I may have no eggs left. I don't want to go down the road of IVF. This is really the best option, and seeing how I'm not young and dumb, I can handle it on my own.

"Well, whatever you need from me, I'm here," Catherine says, offering her support.

"I appreciate it."

"What happens next?"

I lean back in the beach chair and let the sunshine beam down on me. "I find me a baby daddy."

chapter three

ASHTON

"**A**RE YOU SURE ABOUT THIS?" CLARA, THE LEAD reproductive endocrinologist, asks as we sit in her posh office.

I never noticed how pretty it is outside of the lab. We're one of the top infertility clinics in the country, and the lab looks like a damn dungeon. Clara's office is clean but still soft looking and inviting. The white isn't stark, and it's broken up by gold and contrasts of green.

I make a note to tell my boss I want to makeover the lab.

"Ashton?" Clara snaps her fingers, bringing my attention back to her.

"Oh! Yes, I'm sure."

"Okay, then. There will be some rules about what you are and aren't allowed to do regarding the lab work."

I nod. "I figured."

"I have to say, I didn't expect you to be on my schedule to-day." She smiles, her dark brown colored eyes are filled with amusement and wonder.

The look on her face when she saw that her three o'clock consultation was me was priceless. I don't know why she was so damn surprised, though. I've always talked about my desire for a family. This wasn't exactly the route I was planning to take to get there, but life is all about finding a way to pivot.

There isn't a question in my mind as to where I should go. Not because I work here and I'm hoping for a very deep discount—our rates truly are awe-inspiring—but because we really are the best. Clara has gone to great lengths to make sure that we are on the cutting edge of new methods.

Not to mention, I'm pretty damn good on my end.

"Really?"

"I know it's always been your goal to have kids, but it's been a while since you mentioned it."

I sort of gave up on the idea. "Quinn and I didn't work, I'm done wasting time, you know?"

"I understand. So, do you have any questions? I know you know the whole process, but on this side, it's a little different."

I have a million of them and even more fear that I won't be able to conceive. My family may be insanely huge, but I'm an only child. My mother went through hell to have me. It was trouble conceiving, many miscarriages, drugs, tears, and I was a miracle for them. IVF wasn't advanced at that time, so the fact that I didn't come out with three arms was a blessing. There was no clear answer as to why Mom couldn't carry a child, just that her body wouldn't allow it. While a lot of what we know is heredity, my grandmother had no problems procreating.

I've had this fear that I'll be like her. I've already felt a loss for no real reason.

Sometimes it's the one thing we want the most in life that is out of our reach. Immediately, my mind goes to Quinn. I wanted him to give in to his heart and allow us to live our lives together, but that didn't happen.

Now I have to live mine.

"I worry."

"Because of your family history?"

I nod. "And about the selection of donors. I don't really know how that part works."

She smiles warmly. "We have a great collection of men to choose from. They're all screened extensively, and we have a lot of safeguards in place."

"I know that, I just mean, how the hell do I pick one?"

Clara leans forward, hands clasped in front of her on the glass desk. "Well, you read their bio and find someone you think has the best genetic traits that you'd like to see in a child. Also, look at their likes and dislikes, weigh it against what you also feel passionate about. This is your chance to find someone who meshes well with you in all aspects. If I had to do it, that would be my criteria. You sort of get to build your dream baby without having to go through the dating ritual."

"I wish I could meet them . . ."

"You and I both know that's not an option."

"I know, I know, I'm just saying it. There's something about knowing the guy that would make it less . . . clinical."

I look away because Quinn sneaks into my thoughts. I wanted so badly for us to have a child. He or she would've been beautiful. With his shade of blue eyes and perfect body paired with my red hair . . . I could see the dream so clearly. But that's all it is, a dream that I created.

"Have you talked to him?" Clara and I have worked together for a long time. She knows all about my dating woes and Quinn.

My eyes snap up, and I shake my head quickly. "Nothing. He's deployed, so I don't expect to. Plus, we didn't exactly end things with a promise to see each other again. It was sort of the total opposite, actually."

"I was rooting for you guys. I hoped he was going to choose you."

"Yeah, me too. The sad part is that, had he talked to me about it, I would've been okay. I wanted a partner." At least, I believe that's the truth.

Him wanting to serve our country wasn't the issue. The broken promises of what he assured me would come if I just waited for him. I abandoned any opportunity of loving someone else. For three years, I did what he asked. I was understanding, patient, flew there when he couldn't make it to me. Each time, I told myself not to fall harder because it would hurt to leave him. I never wanted to experience what Catherine had when Jackson was shot. I didn't want to be like Natalie when she thought Aaron was killed. As strong as people think I am, I could never endure loving someone and losing them like that.

So, I kept my feelings for him hidden from even myself.

I was an idiot.

I fell so deeply in love with that stupid man, and now look where I am. Knocking myself up.

"You're sure you want to do this now? Do you think there's a chance you can work it out when he returns?" She smooths her ebony hair to the side and waits.

No matter how much I wish there could be, there's not. He would have to admit he has a heart and that it beats, and I'm not holding my breath on that.

"I doubt it. I'm just ready to move on."

Clara clears her throat. "All right."

A tear falls, and I feel like an idiot as I brush it away. "Sorry," I say, shaking off the fresh wave of pain that comes with thinking of Quinn. "I'm happy. I really am. Right now I'm sort of . . . processing."

She smiles. "I understand. It's emotionally straining to even get this far, you know that. The next step is to do a full work-up, exam, and then develop a plan that works for you, okay?"

Clara is the best. She's brilliant, beautiful, and has a kind heart. It's honestly one of the main reasons I continue to work here. We have a very good rhythm and she never pulls punches. If there's an issue, she tells you and then goes to work to fix it. There's never any drama and she likes to face things head on.

There's not a challenge she won't accept.

We're total opposites in every way, but we are the perfect combination. She grew up in a gang-ridden area of New York City, raised by her single father after her mother took off. Clara could've fallen right into the pattern so many have with the violence around her, but she fought against it and earned herself awards and accolades other doctors only dream of. Including being the first African-American woman to earn recognition from both major reproductive organizations in America.

Having her on my side with this is everything.

"Sounds great. When?"

"I have time for the exam now, if you want to get started right away?"

"Really? Yes! Of course!"

Clara's eyes fill with warmth, and I relax a bit.

The door that slammed in my face has been unlocked.

It's not opened yet, but we're getting there.

For the last six months, I've been in a rut. Now, I know what I want, I have a plan, and I'm going to get it.

chapter four

ASHTON

"Ma!" I YELL AS I ENTER THE HOUSE. "YOU HOME?"

"In the kitchen!"

Our family dinners are the only requirement my mother has of me. She doesn't care that I moved to New York or that I'm a fancy baby maker. To her, I'm just her daughter, and that means I move heaven and Earth to get my butt in this house on Sunday afternoons.

Being away at college was an understandable excuse, after that, it was only acceptable if I was traveling. Even then it was a bit dicey because she firmly believes that I should be home on Sundays. However, I don't actually travel, I only say I do because she exhausts me and I need a break sometimes.

"Hey," I say as I enter the room that hasn't changed since I was six. It still has the dark wood paneling that matches the floor and the drop ceiling that I hate. It's old, but homey. My parents bought this house from my mother's parents, and the only update they have done is to install new countertops.

If it were me, I would've gutted the entire house.

I walk over and kiss her cheek, but when I pull away, she grabs my face. "Look how tiny you are. You're working too hard and not eating enough."

My mother is the best. She's about four foot eleven and continues to tell everyone she's really five foot, but we know the truth. Her once brownish-red hair has turned silver, but each week, she's at the beauty parlor getting it done and covering any of her "glitter." She also blames me for each gray hair on her head.

"I'm not working too hard, and I'm not losing weight," I tell her as I wrap my arms around her shoulders.

"You need to eat more."

"I eat enough."

"Look at you," she says with her Jersey accent thickening. "You're all skin and bones. Here, eat some bread."

I roll my eyes. "I'm going gluten-free."

The look of horror on her face is worth it. "You're what?"

I fight every part of me that wants to smile and give it away. "I hear it's bad for you, so I'm not going to eat it anymore. No more bread or pasta," I say while looking over at the pot. Sure enough, there's the spaghetti cooking. "I'll just be eating chicken and vegetables from now on. Do we have chicken?"

Her lips are parted and she keeps shaking her head. "What are you saying? What about all of this food? You love pasta."

"I can't eat it, Ma. You don't want me to do anything that would make me sick, right?"

"I-I—of course not . . ." She pats her hands down her apron. "I'll make you some chicken."

She turns around and now I feel bad. It was funny before, but she looks so sad that I can't keep this going. "I'm kidding, Ma!"

She slaps my arm. "Oh, you're such a brat."

I shrug and grab the piece of bread. "I get it from Daddy."

"Yes, your father is a pain in my ass, just like you are."

"But you love us."

"God only knows why."

I kiss her cheek again and then sit in the chair. Each week, I offer to help cook and each time she tells me to sit. So, I'm skipping the first part. This is how she expresses her love, and I love her for it.

"How are you?"

"Good," she smiles. "I went and visited this morning with Mrs. Burke. She misses Gretchen so much. I hope you never up and move on me."

My mother and Gretchen's are very close. Gretchen's family is as insane as mine and have forced Sunday brunch. I say forced because we don't get to miss if you're related to them. When we were kids, I would go to Gretchen's house and then she'd come to mine.

"I'm sure you'd survive if I left. But I have no plans to go anywhere." Not since my love life is in the crapper and I'm going to need my parents once I'm pregnant. I glance around, noticing there are more chairs than usual. "Who else is coming?"

"Your Aunt Donna and her family, but I'm not sure if your cousins are coming. They've been so busy with work."

I count the seats again. "Okay, but that still leaves three more even if Vinny and the boys don't come."

She nods. "You never know if someone will pop in."

Here we go. My mother . . . the matchmaker. "Mom, who else did you invite?"

"No one, Ashton."

"I don't believe you."

"Oh, fine." She huffs. "I invited some of the ladies from church, but I doubt they'll come."

I toss my head back, groaning at the ceiling. "And their sons?"

She stirs the sauce, ignoring me.

"Mom?"

"I don't know if they'll bring their sons."

"Why do you do this to me? I don't want to date anyone!"

"Because your mother loves you and wants you to know what it's like to be euphorically happy in a marriage," Dad says and then kisses my temple. "Like I make her."

I laugh. "Right. You're such a peach."

Mom scoffs. "Yeah, a rotten one."

He walks over to my mother, wrapping her in his arms and putting his nose in her hair. It makes me want to cry. They have a love like I can only dream of.

"You love me," he says softly.

She leans back, almost as if she can't stop herself. "I do." After a moment, she taps his hands. "Now, let me cook. Go talk to your daughter and find out what trouble she's gotten into this week."

Daddy tilts his head to the side, letting me know we can go to the den to chat.

"So, what's new?"

"Nothing much." I give him the same answer weekly. I could tell him that I'm going to have a baby, but . . . I haven't had any alcohol, and I need to be drunk or already knocked up for that one. That means he won't find out until after I'm actually pregnant.

He will never understand. As wonderful as my father is, he believes you get married and then have babies. To him, the idea that women can go in, get knocked up, and never see or meet the guy they're procreating with is insane. I've listened to it for years, and we've gotten heated a few times.

It's better to be with child, he surely wouldn't kill me then.

"Work good?"

"Yup."

"Good. You have no plans to move back to Jersey?"

I let out a low laugh. "No. Definitely not."

"Fine, fine. Just makes your mother nervous because her little girl is alone in the city."

Yeah, I'm sure my *mother* is truly broken over it. He and I know who the anxious one is, but I let him have his secret. "I'm sure Mom understands that it's best for me."

"Why is that, Ashton?"

"Because I work there, and I need to be away from the circus that resides within these walls."

He shakes his head with a smile. "You were always the independent one in this family. Your cousins wanted to play games, but you wanted to play solitaire. It's not a surprise you wanted to move away."

"Move away? Daddy, I live less than thirty minutes from your house. Catherine moved away. Gretchen moved away. I moved to *Brooklyn*."

"And you'll follow them when Quinn comes back."

"That's never going to happen."

My father loves Quinn. He would sell me if it meant he could adopt that man. Daddy served in the army, and there is no better man than one who gives time to his country. If I told my father that Quinn was a murderer, it probably wouldn't matter. He'd find a way to excuse it. It's the craziest thing.

For years he's held out hope that we'd figure it out and get married. For years, he's been disappointed, just like I have been. Maybe we can form a club?

"Mark my words, pumpkin. That man loves you, and being away makes a person think."

"Oh, I bet he's been thinking, but so have I."

I've thought a lot about how it's not going to be the same again. When he calls, I'm not going to answer. I told him that I was done, and I meant it. There is no point in both of us wasting our time on something that will never change.

There's a time to fight and a time to let go, and I'm very aware of which one I'm at.

"Well, I have hope."

"There are other men, Dad. Ones who aren't afraid of commitment, feelings, making sacrifices for the ones they love."

He releases a throaty laugh. "What sacrifices were you willing to make for him?"

I jerk back. "What?"

"You heard me," Daddy says and waits.

What the hell didn't I sacrifice? "How about my happiness, my wants, my time, my entire freaking life thinking that we were going to have a future. I am not the bad guy here."

"When I talked to him last week, he said that it was you who walked out."

I'm sorry, did he say he talked to him last week? "He told you this when?"

"When he called."

Oh, that clears it up. "I wasn't aware that you spoke to him."

"He calls me once a month. I write him letters because I know what it's like to be deployed."

"Okay, I'm missing something here." I fall back into the recliner, feeling uneasy. How the hell is this even real, and why didn't I know about it? My parents talk to my ex-boyfriend, yet I am just finding this out now? I haven't heard from Quinn in six freaking months. Not a letter, call, email—nothing. But he has time to reach out to my father? "Why do you talk to him?"

Dad leans forward and pats my knee twice. "Because he reaches out to me. I will never turn away a soldier."

"Sailor," I correct. If I had to hear that one more time, I might have screamed. Now, it's apparently ingrained in me.

He laughs. "Right, I forget those squids are particular about their titles. As it seems you are about protecting it."

"It's out of habit, not care."

"Sure it is," Dad says around a knowing grin.

"Still, you didn't answer me, why do you talk to Quinn? You do know we're not together."

"I'm aware."

"Okay?"

I feel like this is a mutiny.

"Okay, what? I like the boy and he needs someone. His father took off when he was young. He barely talks to his mother, and I think every man needs another man to have in his corner."

"I'm your daughter, aren't you supposed to be in my corner?"

My father seems to ponder that and then shrugs one shoulder. "He's my brother in arms . . . I side with the SEAL. Besides, you have more people on your side than you can count."

"Unreal."

Dad chuckles. "That's my middle name."

I know what he's saying is right. I have so many friends, cousins, and family members that I would be hard-pressed to count them all, but only because he doesn't have any, it doesn't mean my father shouldn't side with me.

"Well, I'm glad that you're his new biffle since you're clearly not mine."

He's heard that phrase for years since that's what I've called Catherine since grade school. I always found the acronym BFF stupid. I much prefer a word.

Dad scoffs. "Don't be dramatic."

I roll my eyes and release a heavy sigh. We could argue for days about this, and it'll do no good. Dad is even more stubborn than I am when I think I'm right.

Time to change the subject to neutral ground. "So, who did Mom sucker into coming as my possible date today?"

He shakes his head while looking at the ceiling. "I haven't a clue. The last bozo she brought around was a real winner, huh?"

That was such a disaster. I couldn't believe she would ever think that Anthony "the Hitman" Desoni would be someone I would date. He's ridiculous. He thinks women should be home, cooking their man a hot meal so when he gets home he's satisfied. After dinner, he explained to my cousin why men should be allowed to keep a mistress. Vinny about threw him out of our house after that.

He's my favorite cousin.

"He needs a therapist."

"Hopefully, this round will be better."

"If I weren't so afraid of her, I would threaten not to come to dinner anymore to get her to stop."

Dad shrugs. "I'm sure she'd double her efforts or fake an illness to get you here."

I smile and lean back. "She's a scary little woman."

"Between her Irish and Italian, I never know which side is going to come out stronger or which will kill me."

Considering that my father is full-blooded Italian, he'd probably fall victim to her Irish side.

"She's only Italian when she's sweet."

"She's Irish when she's drunk."

Dad chuckles. "Which is when I love her most."

I roll my eyes. "You love her always."

"I do, the Irish, Italian, and everything in between."

God, they're so in love it's almost nauseating.

The doorbell rings, and I sigh. "Do I have to stay?"

"If the guy is that bad, just fake a stomach ache," he whispers as he gets to his feet. "I'll side with you then."

"Gee, thanks for the support, Dad."

I follow, knowing that delaying the inevitable is worse than getting it over with. Mom's arms are raised as she embraces a blonde woman around her age who is an inch shorter than she is. Two guys stand behind them, and they glance at each other before sighing. Clearly, they're as excited as I am about this.

At least they hopefully don't think this is my idea.

"Phyllis, this is my daughter, Ashton."

My manners precede my dislike for this night, and I do what is expected. I step forward, extending my hand. "It's nice to meet you."

She smiles, taking my hand in both of hers. "You're just as your mother described. These are my sons, Michael and Paul."

How biblical. "Nice to meet you both."

The one nudges his brother, and I could kill my mother. I haven't gotten a look at the guy in the back, but the one who reaches for my hand is at *least* ten years younger than I am. I'm not even sure he's out of college. What the hell is she thinking?

"Nice to meet you. I'm Paul."

I keep my smile in place as I turn to the other guy.

Well, he at least looks to be my age. He's tall with dark hair and a lean body, which is nothing like Quinn's. This guy, who I'm assuming is Mike, has deep green eyes that are almost the color of emeralds, and his smile is warm and welcoming. Quinn's eyes are more of a denim color, and smiling isn't usually what he prefers to do with his mouth.

Great, I did it again.

"Ashton," I say, trying to focus on the man in front of me.

He's not Quinn. Quinn is gone. He's not my man or my friend or anything other than some idiot who has made my dad his new biffle. I will not think of him again from this point forward.

"I'm Mike. It's nice to meet you, Ashton."

His brother snorts. "Yeah, you say that now since she's not a dog."

Well, that explains why he was the second one in. I smile. "You thought you'd use your brother as a shield, huh? Wasn't sure if you were about to meet a Cyclops?"

Mike nods with a grin. "My mother is of the mindset that I should be married, no matter what the girl . . . looks like or how many eyes she might have."

"For the man who is supposed to be my hero, it isn't very brave to send your brother in first."

He shrugs one shoulder, and his lips press into a thin line. "I had no idea you were in need of rescuing."

"Still, nobility isn't sending your little brother in first."

He rocks back on his heels, his mouth relaxing into an easy grin. "Isn't there some rule about keeping the higher ranks behind for strategy?"

This is sort of fun. If nothing else, this guy could become a friend. He's able to banter, and Lord knows I need that in my life. All my damn friends left me, and I have no one to give shit to anymore.

"Maybe, but doesn't a real leader want to protect his men?"

Mike's smile grows. "And a better leader knows which men are expendable, right, Paul?"

Paul rolls his eyes. "Don't let him fool you, I'd have found a way to make him pay."

"See, that was why I was behind him, so I could protect you if need be."

These guys are hilarious.

"Do you have a plan if such a need arises?" I ask with a playful tone.

Mike taps his chin. "I'm sure I'll think of something. Any tips?"

There's a knock on the door, and I smile. "Well, first you could see who else my mother has decided to throw into the mix as possible competition. Dueling isn't something I'm against."

He smiles, turns, and then opens the door.

Only, when I see who it is, the fun and games I was just enjoying is gone. My heart begins to race, my chest constricts, and I want to run into the newcomer's arms, which is a bad thing.

After a few seconds, his warm voice washes over me.

"*Fragolina*, I've missed you."

And then I remember I hate the bastard.

chapter five

*T*HIS COULD GO ONE OF TWO WAYS, AND BASED ON THE LOOK in her eyes, it's not going to be good. Not wanting to have her slap me or maim me in any way, I grab the crutch I leaned against the house so I could knock and tuck it under my arm. If she knows I'm injured, maybe she'll take pity on me.

Her eyes widen, and she steps closer to me. "What happened?"

"I'm fine."

"That's not what I asked," Ashton says quickly. "What happened?"

"Ashton, are you . . ." Her mother's eyes meet mine. "Quinn?"

"Hi, Mrs. Caputo."

"Oh! Quinn is back!" she says with a huge smile. At least someone is happy to see me.

Ashton turns her head quickly, her red hair flowing around her. "I need a few minutes." She doesn't give anyone time to say anything, she just heads out the door, forcing me to limp backward a little as she closes it behind her.

Then we are standing on the porch, watching each other.

I had a plan. I was going to come here, tell her how I feel, and clarify everything, but the words won't come.

"Are you going to explain yourself or stand there and look at me?" she asks with acid in her tone.

I'd be fine with option number two if it meant she wasn't pissed. "I was in an accident."

Her eyes are filled with fear, even though I'm here and I'm fine. "What kind of accident?"

"I can't tell you too many details."

"Of course you can't," she says with exasperation and then looks away. Her wide eyes snap back to mine. "What about Liam? Was he hurt?"

"No, Liam is fine. He wasn't with my squad this time."

I thank God for that. Liam Dempsey is my best friend, and I would never be able to face his wife, Natalie, again if anything ever happened to him. He and I have been through hell and back together. Despite hating each other during BUDs, we're thick as thieves now. There's no better man than him.

"But you're hurt?"

"I sustained minor injuries in the Humvee. Trevor and Bennett are worse than me, but . . . we lost King."

She nods once before clutching her stomach. It's her tell. The thing that always lets me know she's afraid or hurting. As though by holding her stomach, she can keep herself together.

"God, and poor Tessa." Her eyes fill with tears. "They were supposed to get married soon."

The sound of her voice breaks something in me. She shifts a little and I wonder if she is thinking how it could've been me. When her lip quivers, I want to comfort her, but I know it wouldn't be welcome. It's enough that she cares. A part of her still cares about me. I cling to it.

"Hey," I say as I tuck my finger under her chin. "I'm fine."

"No you're not. You're hurt and home early from deployment."

"I missed you." Not exactly what I planned to say first, but it's true regardless.

I do miss her. She is on my mind constantly. Thank God for photos being on cell phones because if I'd had a paper one, I would have worn it out. Before I went to sleep, I saw Ashton. When I woke up, it was her face I wished I could see.

Every single minute, I fought the urge to call her. I just kept hearing her say goodbye in my head over and over and couldn't do it.

That was before the accident.

"Quinn . . ." She steps back, shaking her head. "We're not doing this. I'm not going to . . ."

"Are you with someone?"

I'll fucking die. Of all the things I can't handle, it would be that. Her dad didn't mention it when we chatted, but that doesn't mean anything.

"What?"

"Are you with someone?" I repeat.

"I heard you, but I didn't think it warranted an answer since you broke up with me and it's none of your damn business."

"I didn't break up with you, you left."

This is going all wrong. I need to shut my mouth before I piss her off so much that she won't even hear me out, but the idea of her and another man makes me want to rip someone's head off.

She laughs while shaking her head. "You're a fucking asshole. You want to argue the semantics of our split? Fine, I left you. Poor, Quinn. He had his rotten, black heart ripped from his corpse of a chest. Yes, let's all cry now."

And I did it without even trying. "I'm sorry. I was just caught off guard with finding you and your new boyfriend inside. I assumed you were—"

"I was what? Alone and pining for you? Sorry to disappoint."

I'm a fucking idiot. I knew better. She's the goddamn sun, so of course, she'd find someone else to rotate around her. Who doesn't want that? What man could look at her and not fall to his knees? The fact that I was ever able to escape her gravity, even for a short time, was a herculean effort. I thought I could stay away. Yet, here I am standing before her . . . clearly, I'm not as strong as I think.

"I'd like to meet him," I say.

"Meet who?"

"That guy inside, the one who answered the door, you're with him, right?"

Her eyes widen and then close, not allowing me to see anything. "No, I'm not with him. Not that you deserve an answer, but I'm not cruel."

That's the first bit of good news I've had. "I know I don't, but so much happened, and I needed to see you."

"Why?"

"Why, what?"

She crosses her arms over her chest. "Why did you need to see me? We ended things. You don't want a wife or kids. You don't want to settle down or change your life. We've had this discussion, and you coming around now is a real dick move."

There's nothing I can say that will fully explain what happened this deployment because my entire life has shifted in a way that I can't even grasp. Everything I thought I knew turned out to be a falsehood I created to survive.

Now that it's shattered, I see the truth.

"I know you think that . . . but it's different now."

"I can't go down this rabbit hole again. I'm sorry that you're hurt and that you lost King, I really am, but this isn't going to work. You should head back home."

I'm not leaving her. I won't let this happen again. "No."

"I'm sorry, did you say no?"

"I'm staying. We belong together, Ashton. I know it, you know it—hell, even your dad knows it."

Ashton lets out a laugh. "You know it, huh? *Now* you suddenly know it? Where were you six months ago when I asked you to love me? Where were you a year ago when we fought about our future and you made me promises? Where was this profound knowledge when I told you that I want to get married and have babies and you said—" She taps her chin like she's thinking hard. "'Well, good luck with that, *fragolina*, I hope you're happy with that man.'"

She may be spitting the words at me, but I hear the pain. I hurt her. So many times, I've made mistakes, but I was protecting her from loving me.

"I was a dick."

"Oh, I know."

"I was scared, but I'm not anymore."

Ashton shakes her head. "Well, I'm not yours anymore."

That's where she's wrong. She *is* mine. She will always be mine. "I'm not walking away this time, Ash. No matter how hard you push."

She laughs once. "Good for you, but I'm done. I'm moving on. I have plans, *big ones*, and they don't include going for another ride on the relationship train with you. I'm done being a casualty of that train wreck."

The many arguments I've already prepared start to resurface, but I stifle them. I know that winning her back isn't going to take words, she needs me to prove it. So, that is exactly what I plan to do.

"I have no plans of that either."

"What exactly is your plan then? Did you think I would sleep with you?"

That wouldn't be a bad thing, but I know her better than that. "No, but if you'd like to, I won't turn you down."

She huffs. "Asshole."

I am, but I know sarcasm and anger are her fall backs. If I can evoke those, I'm partially there.

"Let's go inside and have dinner. That's all I'm asking." I know it's a long shot, but maybe she'll take pity on me. "Please. I am injured and all . . ."

Ashton isn't one to give in. It's one of the things I love about her. She's strong, and when she makes up her mind, that's it.

I also know that her heart is ten times bigger than she'd like to pretend it is.

"Don't use that on me."

"Okay, how about I missed you. I came home yesterday and drove here to see you. I would get on my knees and beg for your forgiveness, but I kind of can't."

"Quinn . . ."

"I'm serious. I want to have dinner and then talk."

We stare at each other, waiting for the other to break. I'll be damned if it's me. I've done it to her too many times. I've walked away, given her a reason to think I'll do it again, but this time, I won't.

I love her.

I love her so much that I can't fucking breathe without her. When she left me, I thought I could get over it. In time, I assumed things would be easier. At no point was I prepared for the never-ending pain that would come with knowing I'd really lost her.

I said as much in the letters I wrote but never sent because I knew she'd be the one left hurt. I saved them all and decided to man up and tell her in person. She deserves that much.

"Let the man in." Ashton's father's voice breaks the stand-off. "Quinn, son, come in and eat."

As much as I want to stroll past her and do just as he asked, I have to let it be her.

Ashton whips her head around. "No, Dad. No way. If he stays, then I'm leaving."

"Let the man have a home-cooked meal, pumpkin."

I seriously love her family right now. Although, I suspect she doesn't.

"He can have all the food he wants, but you'll have to tell Mom why I'm leaving."

I missed that fire. It breathes inside her, and when she lets it out, everyone around her burns. It's a thing of beauty so long as you're not in its path.

"It's okay, Ash." She turns back to me, her hands are at her sides but they are clenched in fists. "Mr. C., as much as I'd love to stay, I think it's best if I go." Her eyes widen. "My leg is bothering me a bit, and I plan to do some walking tomorrow in New York."

"You're staying in New York?" Ash asks as she crosses her arms.

"I am. I have this person in the city who I want to see over the next few weeks."

Mr. Caputo smiles. "All right, don't be a stranger, though. Ashton . . ." He turns his gaze to her. "Don't be too long, your mother is starting to pace."

"Sure thing, Dad." Ashton huffs. Her blue eyes turn their focus back to me. "Weeks? You're spending weeks, as in plural, in New York?"

"Could even be months, I have a lot of groveling to do, and

I have a feeling it's going to take time for this person to come around."

Ashton bites her lower lip and closes her eyes. "Don't do this."

I take a step closer, brushing her lip and smoothing where her teeth touched. "I'll see you tomorrow, *fragolina*. And the next day and the next because it's time I started showing up for you."

I kiss her cheek and hobble down the stairs without looking back. I'm ready for the fight of my life, and no matter what scars I end up with, I won't care as long as I win her back.

chapter six

ASHTON

I SLEPT LIKE COMPLETE SHIT.

My night was filled with dreams of my mother's food since I barely ate dinner, dreams of impending doom that ended in train cars on fire, and dreams of super hot sex with Quinn that had me waking up horny.

All in all, I have a feeling today is going to suck.

I climb out of bed an hour before my alarm and start my day. Once I'm dressed in my favorite plum top and my black leggings, I head to the door. I pause once I get there because, what if he's here?

Do I talk to him? Pretend he's not there?

Damn him for fucking up my new normal.

No, you know what? I am a confident, brilliant, and success-ful woman. I don't have to be afraid of seeing him because I'm stronger than that. I have all that I want—or at least, I'm about to once I get myself knocked up.

Which, I plan to have happen sooner rather than later be-cause nothing says I'm over you like a baby with a new man.

My phone pings and I pray it's not Quinn.

It isn't.

Gretchen: I heard you're knocking yourself up.
Me: Catherine has a big mouth.
Gretchen: I'm sure she assumed you told me already.
Me: Probably. Guess what?
Gretchen: What?
Me: I have big news! I'm going to get pregnant without a man present for it.

Gretchen is the most pragmatic one of us. If anyone is going to understand, it's her.

Gretchen: Wow! That's big news! So glad you told me before I heard about it from someone else. Now that I got that out of the way . . . I'm happy for you. Did you pick the lucky guy yet?

That's the part I'm dreading. The whole browsing the book thing is unappealing. I almost wish she would pick for me. That's not a bad idea, actually.

I head out of the apartment and make my way to the elevator while sending her another message.

Me: No, can you come for a visit this week or next?
Gretchen: I'm sure I could come up. My mother is up my ass about not visiting before the wedding, why?
Me: I need you to find my baby daddy. Lots of lists and pro and con columns.
Gretchen: Oh, this is the best gift you've ever given me.

Her and her lists. I swear, this girl needs a support group focused on curbing the need to make them and check them two hundred thousand times.

Me: You're welcome. See you soon!
Gretchen: Yes! And prepare for a list of questions in your email today.

Shocking. Another list.

I make it to the first floor and out the door without seeing Quinn. My leaving early was a fabulous idea if I do say so myself. Usually, I don't roll into work until later in the day because we don't see patients until the afternoons on Mondays. Not that I ever actually see patients, but I like that I get to take my time most Mondays.

Today, not so much.

I put my earbuds in and start to walk. This is what I love about New York City, the air. Sure, it's filled with smog and God knows what else, but I can just breathe when I'm here. While I'm on a street with thousands of people, I can feel completely alone. The rap music blares in my ears as I sing along in my head.

Blocks pass by, and I'm jamming out without a care in the world.

I turn to cross to the other side of the street, and a hand wraps around my arm, pulling me back and against someone's chest.

"Hey!" I protest and turn to give the asshole a piece of my mind, until I see who the hell it is.

Quinn pulls the headphone from my ear as my heart begins to race. "You almost got yourself killed."

"What?"

"You didn't even look at that car that was turning and almost ran you over."

Confused, I look around, see the two people staring at me, and then look over to the car that's flying down the street.

Shit.

"Well, thank you, but you can release me now."

Quinn's hand tightens slightly, pulling me even closer to his body. "I should, but I don't want to."

"You've done it often enough that you should be a pro by now."

He sighs. "Maybe I've learned my lesson."

I have to remember all of the shit I've been through with him. My resistance to him has never been strong, but I'm going to have to hold on to the little I have. He and I don't want the same things, and there's no way to change that.

He wants war and guns and the adrenaline rush from whatever the hell he does. There will never be a merging where we stand.

"Are you still in the navy?" I ask.

"Yes."

"Did you reenlist?"

His eyes fill with sadness. "I had the papers drawn."

So, that's a yes. He's going to do it, just hasn't yet.

"Do you ever plan to give it up, get married, have kids, or love anyone?"

His fingers start to loosen. "No, maybe, I hope, and I already do."

I shake my head and step back. We are not doing this. I am not going to believe that this time is any different. I take the earbud back from him and put it into my ear, letting the angry rap music fuel me. "We're done. Go back to Virginia."

As much as I'd like to believe he's going to do any of that, he won't. Quinn is determined, and apparently, I'm on the list of things to conquer.

I just have to ignore him and hope he surrenders before I do.

⸙

"So he's there? In New York?" Catherine asks as I sit in the bathroom stall, trying to get my head together.

"Yup."

She laughs. "Well, I can't say I'm surprised."

"He always does this, Cat!" I look at her on the screen as she wipes her eyes. I woke her and don't even feel bad about it. She's the only person who will understand. She walked away from Jackson once.

"You and I both know that these guys are determined when they realize they fucked up."

Jackson's head lifts, and he stares into the camera. "You do know it's early here?"

"Good morning, Muffin. Did I wake you?"

He groans and then kisses Catherine's shoulder. "You know we're on the West Coast."

"I don't care. No one told you to move."

Catherine shakes her head. "It's been years, Ash."

"Doesn't make it any easier."

One day, I'll get over it, just not today.

"Regardless," Jackson grumbles, "Quinn loves you, and he's already asked me about positions at the company if he should ever have the need."

"He what?"

"He called a few weeks ago, asking if he could come work for me if his circumstances changed. It happens a lot when the guys are thinking about transitioning out. Apparently, I'm like fucking Santa Clause when it comes to jobs for the good little SEALs in this community. But, with his interrogation and shooting skills, he'd be a great asset."

I stare at my friends because Quinn would never leave.

He's going to reenlist. So, we're talking about years before that would even be possible, right? "But . . . he doesn't want to get out."

Jackson sighs. "Many of us who get out don't do it because we want to. I was shot and that's why I was booted. Hell, Natalie said Quinn got injured and that's why he's home now. Plus, he hasn't signed the papers yet."

"He's on a crutch, but . . ." I think back to the incident on the street. He didn't have his crutch. He was standing there, holding me without it. "He doesn't even need a crutch! The bastard was just playing with me yesterday! Oh, I'm going to kill him myself. Seriously, he had a crutch when he showed up, and then today, he suddenly doesn't need it?"

How low is that? To use a fake injury. Did he think I was going to forgive him for all the shit over the last few years because he had a fake limp? He's dead.

"Ashton," Catherine calls my attention. "He's not faking it, honey. He was manning up so he could make it through the streets of New York without losing you."

"How do you know?"

She looks at Jackson, who answers. "Because it is what I would do. If my job was to protect the girl I love, there would be no amount of pain I wouldn't endure to make sure I was successful in my mission."

"Protect me?" I laugh. "Please, he has done the opposite of that at every turn."

"You're really stupid sometimes," Catherine says. "As much as I'd love to debate this, I have to pee and you need to go back to work. Just think about this, why would he keep coming back? Why were you the first person he ran to when he was released from the hospital?"

"Because he's an idiot!" I yell.

They both laugh as Cat sits up. "Maybe so, but then again, isn't there a saying about fools in love or some shit?"

She hangs up, and I groan. I hate my friends sometimes. He isn't here because he wants to protect me. He never has. All Quinn Miller has ever cared about is protecting his damn self. And what the hell is he protecting me from? Cabbies and coffee? If he cares about my safety, he would stay away from me.

I head out of the bathroom and run into Clara.

"Hey! I was looking for you," she says.

"You were?"

"Yeah, I wanted to see if we could get some blood work started for you."

Yes. This I can control. The baby and my pregnancy is the priority here, so that's what I want to focus on. Not that stupid boy with his stupid penis and his stupid ideas of getting me back.

"I am still very serious. I just know your caseload is huge."

"It is, but you're my friend, Ash. I want to work on this one. Come on, let's get you to the lab and get things moving."

"Ah, the lab," I say with a hint of wistfulness. "My home away from home."

We catch up on a few cases we're working on as we walk. It's been a tough few weeks for both of us. One of the patients, who should've had no problem conceiving, lost her last viable embryo. It was, by far, one of the hardest cases I've worked on. In the lab, it's easy to be slightly detached since I focus on the science of things and, most of the time, I don't have to see their faces. But Clara and I had spent a lot of time trying to figure out what was happening, and we both grew more and more invested in every loss. It was heartbreaking, really.

"Do you have any worries?" she asks as we approach the lab.

"Just that it won't work. You know my family history and how I worry that I'm going to be like my mother, not to mention my age and the fact that my viable eggs have dwindled."

"I won't lie to you, Ashton, we have no idea yet what the chances are and if you'll be able to carry. We still don't know what exactly caused . . ."

Caused the miscarriage.

Clara is the only person other than Quinn who would know this wouldn't be my first pregnancy. Just about three years ago, I was pregnant with my married boyfriend's baby.

I found out two weeks after I met his wife. I was a mess and had gone to Clara so she could do a full workup. I found out that I was nine weeks pregnant.

I lost that baby two weeks later, and all the fears I had about my inability to have children, became very real.

"I know, but I'm going to hope that was a fluke."

She gives me a sad smile. "I hope so too, and this time, we'll be prepared with great medical care through the entire pregnancy."

There wasn't anything we could pinpoint as to why I miscarried, but Clara had suggested that stress could have been a large factor.

So, after I lost the baby, I took a month off work.

I headed to Virginia Beach and hung out with Mark because I figured he would be someone who wouldn't judge me. Jackson's best friend and I have gotten along from the beginning. He makes me laugh, and for about two seconds, I thought maybe he and I could be something. Thankfully, that idea disappeared as soon as it started.

He's the crazy ass in their group of friends, just like I am. We get along great, but there was never that spark. It was almost like looking into a mirror, and it got old very quick.

Instead, I got a great guy who I can count on as a friend. I also think that, had I ever crossed that line, he never would have met Charlie, the woman he was meant to be with.

"Ashton?" Clara calls my attention back to her.

"Yes?"

"Have you told anyone about this? Any support system in place? I hate to ask, but I think it's more important than we think it is. Most of the success cases have a large number of people there for the triumphs and losses."

"I told Cat."

She nods. "And?"

"And I'm sure she told Jackson. Gretchen also knows."

"What about your parents?"

"Not yet. I want to get through this part first."

We come to a stop outside the door to the lab. "I understand you wanting to wait, and this is me talking as a friend, but if the labs come back and say that it'll be more difficult than we thought, you're going to want someone there to hold your hand. I'm asking you to think about it, that's all."

If it goes down that road, I won't need a hand to hold, I'll need someone to hold me together.

It's just that the person I would want is the last person I will ever tell.

chapter seven

ASHTON

I HAVE NEVER BEEN MORE PHYSICALLY EXHAUSTED THAN I AM right now.

It's eight o'clock, and I'm just leaving the office. There was an issue with one of the freezers that house the frozen eggs, and my team and I worked fast and tirelessly to make sure we lost nothing.

Thank God we have alarms set to warn us about temperature variations.

At least the chaos of my afternoon helped keep my mind busy. My test results will be back in a few days, but I have what I'm calling the "Baby Daddy Book" in my bag. Clara said it's best to start combing through it now and at least narrow down the options.

I love shopping, but this is a whole new version of a catalog.

I step outside, cracking my neck and breathing in deep. Not only did I come into work earlier than I normally would but also I'm leaving later, and I missed my spin class. Oh, and I had three crackers for lunch.

"You okay?"

I jump at the sound of Quinn's voice. "Jesus!"

"Usually, you would call me God."

Idiot. "What are you doing here? No—" I stop and shake my head. I don't need this today. "You know what? I don't care or want to know. You're just some creepy guy on the street, and I don't talk to creepy guys." I don't wait for a response before I stick my earbuds in, turn the music up, and tune him out.

There's no doubt in my mind that he's following me. He's either been waiting outside my workplace all day or he put some tracking device in my bag. Neither would be entirely surprising.

Right when I'm starting to get lost in the lyrics about fucking the police on my way to the subway, I feel him beside me. I try not to look at him, feel him, smell his cologne amongst the smells around me, but I can't stop it.

Quinn Miller has always been my weakness, damn it.

He pops an earbud out and puts it in his own ear. "Hey!" I protest.

"I wasn't sure what angry rap song you were listening to. I was curious."

"As if that gives you the authority to find out?"

He smiles. "You should get a new playlist."

"There's nothing wrong with my playlist."

Seriously, some people just don't appreciate the classics of rap. The new stuff lacks the anger and feelings the rappers of the 90s embraced.

"You need to get with the times."

Quinn is baiting me. I know it, and the smirk on his perfect lips tells me that he's enjoying bothering me. One does not mess with me regarding my music.

"I'll take that under advisement. Now, give it back."

"But we're walking."

"No." I huff. "I'm walking, you're stalking. Stalkers usually hide in the bushes or stay out of sight, you should try that."

He smiles. "Thanks for the tip."

I try to ignore him, but it's really hard. Quinn is a big guy, almost six foot three, stocky, but it's not just his size, he bends the space around him, making it conform. Quinn has this way that makes it impossible to not be aware of his presence.

Yet, when he wants to be invisible, he's somehow able to do that. Right now is not one of those times.

He *wants* me to be completely aware of him.

As we walk the few blocks to my station, I try to let the lyrics hold my focus but continue to glance over at him.

He doesn't seem at all bothered by me. He's simply walking along as though he doesn't have a care in the world.

Being quiet has never been my strong suit. There's no such thing as comfortable silence in my world. He also knows this. Each step that we take with him keeping his eyes straight, pretending as though I'm not here, is making me fucking crazy.

"Where's your crutch?" I ask after I can't take any more.

"Huh?"

Asshole heard me. "Your crutch. I noticed you're walking fine today."

"I didn't need it today."

"Why is that?"

If he's willing to suffer because of whatever crazy mission he's put himself on, I'm going to injure his other leg for him.

"Because I can't exactly maneuver this city with a crutch. Lord knows you weren't going to slow down."

"Nope. I sure wouldn't. So, if I start to run, you'll . . ."

"Run with you."

I roll my eyes. "You're hurt and you'd run to keep up with me?"

"There's not much I wouldn't do to be close to you right now."

Don't fall for it, Ashton. Don't let him make you think this is more than just his pride.

Even after telling myself that, my chest tightens, my heart races, and a part of my wall cracks a bit. Damn him.

"Too bad you didn't realize how fantastic I was before everything went to shit."

His hand wraps around my elbow, causing me to stop. "I knew how fantastic you were the first moment I saw you, Ash. I've always known. It was that I didn't deserve you or your love."

My eyes lock on his deep blue ones, looking for any sign that he's lying and finding none. The sincerity in his gaze makes it hard to breathe. How I wish it was a few months ago because it would've mattered then.

"And now you are?" I ask, unable to stop myself.

"Now, I'm willing to prove that I can be that man."

I shake my head. "It's too late, Quinn. You and I have been through this too many times. I can't do it anymore. I want more. I want it all. I wanted you to be that man for me, but you closed that door the last time."

I see the regret flash in his eyes. "I know."

"So, why do this now?"

Here on the busy streets of Manhattan, we stand at the corner, as if no one else exists.

Quinn lifts his hand, pushing back a strand of my hair and tucking it behind my ear. "Because I can't walk away again."

It's not his decision anymore.

"I already did. You don't have to. I won't keep trying and begging and hoping that things will work out the way I hope. It's been years of pretending and years of heartache."

"I won't hurt you again," Quinn promises.

I want so badly to believe him. No matter how stupid or how much I wish it was different, my heart is his. I love him beyond all reason, and being this close to him is going to make me do stupid things.

My feet shift back, needing a little distance. "I wish I could believe you."

"I'll just have to prove it."

"Please don't do this," I implore. "Walk away before either of us forgets the hell we've put each other through."

Quinn moves in, not allowing me the space I want. His voice is soft and pleading. "I want us to forget, Ash. I need to find a way to make you see that it's the past and I can't walk away again."

I release a heavy breath, trying to push out the want to crumble back into his arms. He would catch me, I know he would, but when he pushes me aside, it'll hurt.

"Well . . . that's too bad about your leg, because I can."

And then I walk off, with one less earbud.

I move through the crowds, twisting and turning so I can get away. I'm too worn out today to deal with him. Whenever I decide to battle with Quinn, I have to have my full wits about me. He's smart, knows me, and can wear me down too easily.

When I get to the next red light, I cross the street, knowing that, if I stop, he'll catch me.

"You could slow down a little," he says now occupying the space I wish he wasn't.

"Damn it!" I stomp my foot. "You can't even give me this?"

"I told you, I'm not letting you go."

"No," I clarify, "you said you weren't walking away, which is what I did. You're just following me."

He laughs once. "This is true. I'll clarify. I love you. I'm not walking away, letting you walk away, giving you up, or doing anything that even comes close to ending with us not being together."

My heart is pounding so hard I can't be sure I heard anything after his second sentence. I stare at him, wondering if he knows what he said or if maybe I am making it up.

"What did you say?"

"I said I wasn't letting you go."

I shake my head. "Yeah, I heard that, you said something before it."

He takes my hand in his. "I love you."

"That was what I thought you said."

"I didn't plan to say it like this."

I never anticipated hearing it. In all this time, he's never uttered those three words—as though saying them would weaken him in some way. Natalie explained it once, saying that if they pretend to be these big, strong, unfeeling men that it's easier for them when they leave. She said that she and Aaron would fight before a deployment so it was easier for him to leave.

In some ways, I can understand that, but then, what the hell has changed?

"What did you plan?"

When someone pushes him from the side, he moves a little closer to me, shielding me with his body. I guess Jackson was right about Quinn trying to protect me.

"I wanted us to sit down at a dinner, and I was going to explain it all. I should've known that you would never agree to that or make it easy."

I scoff. "Because you've made anything easy on me?"

"No, and that's why I never should've thought it should be for me."

I rub my head, feeling the beginning of a headache coming on. "I don't know what to say."

"Don't say anything. Just walk home and know I'm right behind you in case you need me."

He's making it really hard to hate him. "Maybe you can walk with me . . ."

"Is that what you want?"

Yes. No. Maybe. No. I have an inner war with myself and decide whatever the next thing out of my mouth is the truth. "Maybe." I don't feel any better about that answer.

"It's better than no."

"It's not a yes," I clarify.

"It will be," he says with self-assuredness that makes me want to throat punch him.

"Don't be so sure."

Quinn leans in so that his lips barely brush against my ear. "I know you too well. I know your eyes, your body, and your thoughts even when you think you're hiding them. You and I both know that as much as you want to deny that, you can't."

I grab my earbud from his hand. "Well, my maybe has been switched to a no."

"That's fine. I'll be right behind you, waiting for you to turn around and see that I'm ready for whatever it is you want."

And then the petty part of me comes out in full force. I laugh because he will never be ready for what I want. He only thinks he does, and the sooner I can get it through his thick skull, the better. "You think you'll be here for whatever I want?"

"No, I *know* I will."

So he thinks. "Well, in nine months when my baby is born, I guess we'll see where you are."

Before he can say a word, I walk away, leaving him stunned as I take the stairs to my train.

chapter eight

QUINN

"**S**HE'S PREGNANT?" LIAM ASKS AS I SIT IN MY RENTED APARTMENT in her building, trying to fucking make sense of what she said.

"It seems so."

"Who's the father?"

That's the million-dollar fucking question. Some asshole touched her. Another man has been inside her, where only I belonged. I was a fool to think it wouldn't happen. I knew there was a possibility of her moving on, but I never anticipated this.

"I don't know, and I don't care."

Liam laughs. "Right. You don't care."

"I don't," I toss back. Sometimes, I question our friendship. Not that either of us wouldn't lay down our lives for the other. Not that our friendship isn't rock solid, but I wonder why the hell he likes me.

He's loyal, kind, and would do anything for anyone. I'm a bastard who fucks up everything.

"You're either the dumbest asshole I know or the biggest liar. You wouldn't have told me to call you from the sandbox if you didn't care."

He's the only one I trust enough to talk to about this. So, yeah, I told him to call me from the deployment and then I sent the dickhead forty bucks for the call online. At least he can't call me cheap.

"I didn't say I don't care that she's pregnant," I inform him. "I don't give a shit who the mother fucker is she screwed."

Again the asshole laughs. "The hell you don't. How about you stop bullshitting me and yourself. You care because you love her. I don't know when the hell you finally got your head out of your ass, but here's the thing . . ." He pauses and releases a heavy sigh. "You have a choice. You can be a man and go to her. Do the opposite of what she expects, which is for you to act like an idiot. Or you can live up to her expectations."

"I'm not you, Liam."

"What does that mean?"

It means I'm not a good man like he is. I can't step into another man's family and do right by them. He's that guy. He walked into Natalie's life and picked up the pieces. There wasn't any hesitation where he needed to go back and think about it. No, he dug in and loved her and her kid.

"Just what I said."

"Oh," he says with a knowing voice. "You mean that you're not as good as me. We already knew that. Not many are."

"Dick."

"You're so damn busy beating yourself up that you forget the good things you do. Look, I wouldn't be friends with you if you were a piece of shit. That's just me being honest. The choice is yours, Quinn. If you lose her, then it's because you let her go. If she loves someone else, then you have to love her enough to let her be happy."

I love her more than she'll ever know. Letting her go isn't the issue because I've already done that. It's when I see my life without her that I can't fucking take it. My heart aches each night at the thought of her not being with me. I fight so hard to stay away, and I always find myself on her doorstep.

My eyes close, and my head falls back. "So many things I would've done differently."

"I get that. Regrets are a man's worst nightmare."

Chief says that before every deployment. We have a team meeting where we find out a little about what our missions and goals are, and then he tells us to go home and wrap up all our loose ends. He always says that it's not what you do before you leave that'll fuck your head up, it's what you don't do.

According to him, having regrets is the highest cause of casualties.

"It wasn't until the accident that I understood that saying."

"Yeah, almost dying will do that to you."

Liam and I talked about this before I left to head back to the States. I explained the conversation I was having with Trevor, King, and Bennett before the Humvee accident. The four of us were laughing, talking about how King was going to get married when he got back. We were joking about how he wouldn't be the king of anything anymore because he was about to be shackled.

Only he didn't look sad about any of it. In fact, he smiled at the idea of marrying Tessa. He was happy because he never questioned her love and she was willing to put up with his shit.

Then, in the midst of him explaining how love wasn't a shackle, we were airborne.

"I can't stop seeing his face. I can't help but wonder if he felt like he missed out by not marrying Tessa sooner. Then all I could think about was Ashton. I knew that, if I died, I would regret letting Ash walk away. It was all there, and I have to fix this."

Liam is quiet for a few seconds. "If I died, I would have no regrets. I know that my wife loves me and is very much aware of how I feel about her. My kids are everything to me, and they know it as well. You've spent your entire adult life worried about what would happen to the people around you if you died that you forgot to live."

"I've done what I thought was right."

"Yeah, and how's that working for you?"

To think I called him for support. "You should be a motivational speaker, Dreamboat, or maybe a therapist because you're super fucking helpful."

He snorts with a low chuckle. "No, I'm honest. You don't need me to blow smoke up your ass, buddy. You've been doing that to yourself for long enough. I'm not going to lie because, if I remember correctly, you didn't do it when I was dating Lee. So, I'm going to say this and then I'm going to hang up because my wife is waiting for me to call. If you love Ashton, then figure out what you need to do to show her. If you can't love her and the baby she's carrying, walk away and nurse your broken heart away from her. She's going to be a mother now, and she doesn't need to take care of you along with a kid."

"Thanks for the advice, asshole."

"Anytime, douchebag."

I disconnect and head to the window. The place I found is a few floors above hers and it would be so easy to go to her, but I won't do that until I know for sure what my plan is. Liam is right, her life is about to change, and I've caused enough issues to last her a lifetime.

I stare out at the skyline and wonder if I could walk away if I wanted to.

I know that I couldn't.

Now, I just need to get off my ass and get my life together.

chapter nine

ASHTON

I DID IT. I PUSHED HIM AWAY. I KNEW IT WOULD HAPPEN WITH those few little words, and even though that was my goal . . . I wanted to be wrong.

He said he loves me. For the first time, those words escaped his lips and my world tilted just a bit.

Then he didn't chase me, and that tilt became nothing but broken ground beneath my feet.

It's almost ten, and while I wish I could fall asleep, there's not a chance in hell it'll happen. I grab my workbag and a glass of wine and flop onto the couch. Since there's nothing else to do, I might as well browse the book before I chicken out.

I'm not sure what parameters to look for, though. Obviously, I want someone who is in good health and smart. There are a few types of smart—book and street—and I can't exactly tell if a guy has common sense based on his bio, but I want the father to be someone I might have chosen if he and I met.

I flip each page slowly and sip my wine, but when I'm about halfway through, I groan.

Not one guy has appealed to me.

I blame Quinn. If he hadn't shown up, the firefighter with the tight ass would've been perfect.

Knock, knock, knock.

I jump, almost spilling my wine. Who the hell is at my door this late? I didn't order food so there are really only a few other possibilities. One is that my stupid ex-boyfriend has come out of his statue-like state—three hours later—and wants to talk. Another is that it's someone who doesn't know what apartment they're at. Three is that it's a hero with an impressive dick who is going to save me from the hell of picking a sperm donor.

Knock, knock, knock.

Well, whoever it is, they don't possess the gift of patience.

I get up, grab my bat that sits by the front door because the asshole superintendent painted our doors including our peepholes, and open it.

"You're like a cockroach!" I say with exasperation when I see Quinn, who I was hoping it wasn't.

"That would've been a good call sign."

I roll my eyes. "I think you live up to yours pretty well, Ladykiller. You killed a part of me."

Quinn steps forward, eyeing the bat. I raise a brow in challenge because I'm not afraid to hit him. Maybe it would knock some sense into the asshole. Though, we both know he could have the bat out of my hand and have me tossed on the floor with my arms behind my back before I could lift the damn thing.

"I never wanted to."

I sigh and push the door open. "Might as well come in."

He enters my apartment and looks around, always surveying the scene.

At first, I couldn't understand it, but after Catherine explained that it's their training, I found myself doing it too.

I know where the exits are, I hate sitting with my back to the door, and I'm always paying attention to little things.

What he sees is that I haven't cleaned in a week and still haven't unpacked from my trip to California. Besides that, everything is still the same. I haven't changed or done much of anything since I moved in.

Finally, he looks at me with a smile. "The only thing I hope to kill is the hatred you have toward me."

"I don't hate you. That's the issue."

Quinn's head bobs as he moves around. "You don't love me, that's also the issue."

If he only knew.

"Maybe you should've given me a reason to love you."

Quinn's eyes soften as he stares at me. "I'd like to give you them now."

I sigh and shake my head. "It's too late."

"You keep saying that, but I don't believe you."

He's so damn arrogant some days. Today being one of them. I just wish I weren't getting slightly turned on by it.

There's something wrong with me.

Only I would find him standing here, looking all badass and ready to win me back, sexy. He's the guy who has failed me time and time again.

I sit on the couch and glare at him. "In case you missed what happened on the street earlier, things have changed. We're not the same people anymore. I'm not in love with you, and we both know you're not in love with me."

He smirks. "Do we now?"

"I sure do."

"And what exactly is it that you know?"

"The sheer volume of things would floor you," I say back with sarcasm.

Quinn sits beside me. "Then, feel free to enlighten me."

Fine. "First, you don't love me."

"I disagree," he interrupts.

"Good for you, but it's true."

He shifts closer so his leg presses against mine. "How do you know what's true, Ash? How can you know? I'm here. I'm sitting next to you, even with the information you dropped on the street. I don't care if you're pregnant, I want you."

This is totally backfiring on me, so I change tactics. Quinn is a jealous and possessive guy. I have to make him think there's someone else. "I love the baby's father."

That makes him stop inching toward me. "Don't lie to me, *fragolina*. You already told me there was no one else."

Fuck. I forgot that I said that on the porch. "I lied then."

He laughs once. "Nice try." And then he moves as if he's going to climb over me. The only option I have is to move back to avoid his mouth.

"I don't love you."

"I think you do, but that's for another time."

I'm now lying flat on my back as he braces himself above me. How the hell did I get here? My whole entire mission was to piss him off and make him leave me alone. However, he's doesn't seem to have the same ideas that I do.

Doesn't he see how much it breaks me to be this weak to him? It's exhausting trying to be so strong all the time. My heart is racing and my palms are sweating as I try to formulate a way out of this situation. I could knee him in the balls, but that would be mean. I could yell and push him away, but I don't want to.

"What do you want, Ash?"

You.

I want you.

I'm not strong enough for this. My fingers slide up his back, and he winces. "Quinn?"

"It's fine."

I sit up, shoving him back with me. "Let me see."

Unlike a normal person, he doesn't lift the back of his shirt. No, he pulls it off, giving me the other thing on him I can't resist . . . the perfect view of his washboard abs.

As much as I'd like to ogle him, I can't appreciate the unbelievable shape of his body because there are angry red marks and a bandage right under the tattoo of the frog skeleton on the right side of his chest that wraps around to his back.

"I told you I came home a few days early."

"You just said you were fine."

He leans back, brushing his hand over his face. "And I am fine."

"What happened?"

"An accident."

"Please don't be coy with me. You're hurt . . . more than just your leg. You lost King, and I want to know how you got hurt."

Quinn shifts. "Everything is fine. I don't want to talk about it."

I release a heavy breath, pulling my legs underneath me. We don't talk, and we never have, which is what has put us in this mess to begin with. "This is part of the problem, you know? I want to be here for you, but you don't know how to let me. You say you love me, and I think, somewhere inside you, that's true. But not communicating is not the kind of relationship I want. I used to be okay with it, the secrets and us having separate lives. I understood that you had to protect yourself because of your job. But the more you did that, the more you pushed me out and the more my heart broke."

He jerks back, and I see the anger and fear starting to build. "Because I don't want to tell you all the gory details?"

"I'm not asking for details, Quinn. I'm asking for you to let me in. I'm asking for you to share something with me. Not about the accident, but about what happened."

He gets to his feet, and I wrap my arms around my stomach to keep it together. I have no idea if he's going to tell me or if he's going to walk out.

"I can't tell you."

When our eyes meet, mine are filled with sadness. In a part of my heart, I wanted this time to be different because I do love him. Quinn is the only man I've ever felt this way for. He is my heart and soul, no matter how much I wish it were otherwise.

I stare at him, begging for him to say something, to give me anything. "I don't need it all, I just need a piece."

He shakes his head. "There are no pieces to give."

My heart sinks. "I figured."

"Not because I don't want to trust you but because this is the part of my life I don't think you need to be burdened with. No one should give the woman they love this kind of baggage."

I hate that he feels that way. I wish he would say that it's too heavy for him to carry alone. I want to shoulder it with him. "Do you think Liam or Jackson feel like that? Do you think that Ben or Mark don't share with the women they love? Because I promise you, they do."

His eyes close, dark lashes fall, and I know that he won't crack.

"It doesn't matter."

My lips form into a thin line. "It matters to me. Please, let me be and go."

He groans and grabs his shirt. "I'm not perfect, Ashton. I'm far fucking from it, but I'm here and I'm trying."

"And I appreciate it, but it's not enough to always be on the fringes of your life. I want it all, Quinn. I want a baby, a marriage, a life with a man who is willing to share it all with me."

"I need some time!"

God this is the definition of insanity. "You've had years! Years! I don't have that luxury anymore. I'm having a baby."

"Who is the father?"

I jerk my head back. "None of your business."

His lips purse, and I can practically feel the testosterone rolling off him. "None of my business?"

"Nope. You lost that right."

"Tell me, Ash."

"Why? So you can what? Beat him up?"

He clenches his hands. "I can't do this."

"Can't do what?"

"I can't imagine you with another man."

I'm being such a bitch, but I can't seem to care enough to stop. He has no right to show up and demand anything.

"Leave, Quinn. Just leave and save us both the heartache."

His breathing is so heavy I can hear the effort it's taking him to stay calm. He's said so many times that I'm the only person who does this to him. Part of what he prides himself on is being stoic. Not many people can walk into a room where they know they could die and smile, Quinn can. When he's with me, all that self-control goes out the door, and I love it.

I like that I'm the woman who brings him to his knees. I also like that he's pissed off about a baby that doesn't exist yet.

"No," he says and steps closer. "Not until . . ."

"Not until?"

A long, slow breath exits his lips and then his eyes close. "Not ever."

We both know that statement is not true. He's on leave, and he'll have to go back and then deploy again. Just like every other time before. "You say that, until the navy tells you otherwise."

"I can't change what I am."

A tear falls because he still doesn't get it. "I don't want you to. That's the thing. I loved you so much, and I would've been there if you included me, just once. You make choices without regard for me, and you don't include me, Quinn. You don't want me to be a part of your life, you just want me in it."

"I've changed. I don't want a life without you." His voice is soft, but there's an edge to it. Knowing how much emotions scare him, I know that took a lot of effort.

"You want to marry me?"

The fear flashes, but he recovers quickly. "If that's what you want."

I laugh once. "You can't even say the words."

"Marry me," he says quickly.

"What?"

"You heard me. Marry me. Marry me right now. We'll go to Vegas or wherever you go to get married."

I rear back as if he's slapped me. "Wow, Quinn, why don't you romance me a little harder, you fucking asshole. I don't know that any woman has ever heard such a fantastic proposal before. Nothing says love like a fight with a demand of marriage at the end."

"What do you want, Ashton? Do you want babies? I'll give you a hundred. Do you want your own lab? I'll find a way to build you one!"

"That's not the issue!" I grip my hair and scream. "You're too late. You had every opportunity to love me, build me a lab, or give me a hundred babies, and you chose not to. You discard me every single time. You let me go because it's too hard to hold on. So, no, I don't want to marry you." The tears fall from my eyes freely. I hate that I'm breaking apart in front of him, but I can't stop it. It hurts too damn much.

"What, are you going to marry the guy who knocked you up? You're going to run off with the first guy who does what you want? Even knowing your heart still beats for me? That your breathing accelerates when I'm close because you fucking need me. You can have your child with some guy, but you'll always wish it was with me."

I raise my hand back to slap him, but he grabs my wrist before I can connect. "Get out!"

He releases my hand and touches my cheek with tenderness. "No, *fragolina*. I won't."

I stare at him with a steady stream of tears. "*Why?* Why won't you let me be?"

"Because I love you." His fingers slide across my lips. "You can hit me. You can tell me to leave. You can scream or claw my eyes out or anything else you want, but I'm not leaving you. I've done enough of that. You love me, Ashton, all the asshole parts and the ones that make you crazy because you and I are right for each other."

"Look, you might be some badass navy SEAL who can read people and whatever, but you do a shit job of reading me, and you need to leave before we both say something we'll both regret."

He brings his fingers down my neck. The rough tips trace the slope of my shoulders, making their way lower against my arm to my hand so he can interlace them with mine. "I can read you better than I can read myself. I see you when I close my eyes. I feel you even when I do everything I can not to. Your perfume is fucking embedded in my nose so there's no escaping you."

My heart is racing as his touch and scent surround me. Quinn's lips inch nearer, his blue eyes grow darker the closer he gets. "Don't kiss me."

"Don't fight me."

chapter ten

ASHTON

I TRY TO STEP BACK, BUT INSTEAD OF PUSHING OFF HIM, THE fingers of my free hand wrap around the back of his neck. "I hate you," I say the words without any conviction.

"You love me, and I fucking love you. Kiss me, Ashton."

His hands tangle in my hair, holding me right where he wants me. "No."

"Why not, *fragolina*? What's wrong?"

This. Him. The fact that we're doing this. I should be ignoring him, not all worked up and unable to stay away from him.

"You," I say with the anger that's building. "You being here is what's wrong."

Now I'm beyond pissed. This isn't fair. He is making all of this a problem. When he was in the desert, I was just fucking fine. If he were in Virginia Beach, like he's supposed to be, I would be okay. I could go about my damn day, have my baby, and not think about him. But, no, he won't let that happen.

"Good."

"Good?"

Quinn's lips brush against my ear. "When you're angry,

you're honest, so be pissed off and tell me why you're upset?"
Then he takes the lobe in his teeth, and I would fall if his arms
weren't holding me up. "Is it because you want me? Is it because
you still love me, and now that I'm here . . . you can have me?"

"It's because you're a bastard."

He softly chuckles. "That's true, but I'm the man who is
standing here."

"For how long?"

That's the million-dollar question. He says he's here, but
he's been here before, and I'm well aware of how that turned
out.

"Until you're either coming with me or I've lost you completely. But, either way, you're in for the fight of your life because I'm not running off."

I want to fight. Every part of me wants to reject him, but I
can't. I won't deny him again or tell him to get out. So, I crash
my lips to his in a searing kiss.

It's as though time stops the moment we touch. I hold his
head to mine, pressing my body to his as though he was a tree
and I was the vine. Quinn pulls me tighter as we both drown in
one another.

Our tongues move in tandem, teeth gently biting at the other's lips as we fight for and against for dominance. I can't draw
air in fast enough, but it's okay because he's keeping me alive.
His fingers tangle in my hair, tightening just enough for me to
feel pressure and his need.

There's so much being spoken in this kiss, but I can't think
clearly enough to process it. All I know is that I've missed him.
So many nights I've lain awake, wondering about him, thinking
of how I wished we could be different.

Now, he's here, and I can't let him go.

Quinn lifts me, and my legs wrap around his hips as he lays

me on the couch. "Ashton." He says my name as though it were a prayer. "I love you."

I can't hear those words right now. "Don't say it," I plead and pull his mouth back to mine. Kissing him is all I want.

He hovers over me, hands roaming my sides, brushing right under my breast before moving to cup my face with his rough fingers.

Quinn has man's hands. They're not soft or maintained because he works hard. I missed that feeling. Missed him touching me and making me feel it everywhere. There's no doubt that he's the one branding me with the scrapes from the callouses on his fingers. I can remember each scar from the bullets, knife fights, or whatever else happened that he wouldn't tell me about.

Then reality tries to weasel its way into my bliss. I'm kissing him when I'm trying to get rid of him. Damn him and his ability to scramble my brain.

I need to stop this. I need to get some distance. The scent of him is intoxicating, and in order to get through it, I need my wits about me.

I turn my head and struggle to catch my breath.

"Ash?"

"No," I say as I rest my hand on his chest to keep him from kissing me again. "You're not going to make me feel this way. I'm done. All the way done. I want my life and my heart back. The one you took three years ago. I want to go to a bar, dance with a guy, and maybe take him home. I want to walk through the streets without looking for you or thinking I want you there, because I don't. I want to stop comparing every stupid man to you. You took that all from me! Give it back, damn it!"

He grips my hand, holding it over his chest. "No."

"No?"

"No. I won't give it back because I want every guy to

measure up short. I want you to feel my hands when another man touches you, and I want you not to be able to stand it. You think it's only you who's fucked up from this?" He laughs once. "I'm fucking lost without you. I've lowered myself to getting our friends and family involved. So, no, I won't give anything back."

Asshole. "Stop saying these things! It's too late! It's too much!"

"Then deny it, Ashton. Tell me you don't love me," he demands.

My heart is racing, and my breathing is labored. I want to say it. I could make this all go away with one little lie. It should be so simple because him leaving is what I want, right? It's the way I can move forward with my life. But I hate liars. I hate those who use other people to gain what they want. It's not who I am. "I can't deny it. I just don't want to love you anymore!"

We both move toward each other in a rush. I kiss him, anger mixed with passion whipping around us with so much force that I couldn't stop myself if I wanted to. His lips are all power as he slides his tongue into my mouth.

We may not be right for each other, but there is nothing wrong about this.

He kisses me hard, and I love the feel of his fingers as they wrap around the strands of my hair. Quinn kisses with a power that renders me helpless. It's impossible to resist him.

He moans against my mouth, and my hands press against his hard chest. I want him so much. I want to not want him even more, but I can't stop it. He breaks the kiss, but his lips move to my neck.

"I hate you," I tell him.

"No you don't."

"Shut up."

His warm breath is right against my ear. "You shut up."

"Make me."

He slowly drags his lips back to mine, effectively doing exactly what I told him to do—shut me up.

I can't think when his hands start to roam my side. My head is jumbled with thoughts of how good it feels and how much I want him. When he moves to my stomach and starts up, I know I'm fucked.

I try to buck up, but he grips my hip. "I need to touch you."

I need to stop this. If I don't, there will be no backing out. Then his hand moves higher, brushing against the underside of my breast, eliciting a groan that escapes my lips. "Quinn," I say, not sure what the hell I'm trying to get him to do. Touch me more or stop altogether.

"Let me make you feel good."

God, that's an interesting offer. "And then what?"

His thumb brushes against my nipple. "And then we figure this out."

I'm pretty sure we're supposed to talk first and then have sex, but Quinn and I have never exactly followed any kind of protocol. "One time," I say both to him and to myself. It can only be this once.

He grins. "I much prefer multiples, *fragolina*, and I know you do as well."

And then there are no more words.

His hands are on my skin, and I'm lost to him. His power is intoxicating, and I want to drown in it. He tears my shirt off, revealing my breasts.

He cups them, moving his thumbs against each nipple. Then he moves his hands to my back, pulling me up so he can take me into his mouth. His warm tongue circles my nipple, sucking at just the right pressure before moving to the next. My fingers thread into his hair as he alternates.

Quinn pushes me back onto the couch. The soft leather causes me to shiver as the heat of his body covers me.

He kisses me again, his tongue dueling against mine. Kissing a man like him is an entire body experience.

I sigh against his lips when his fingers move down my shorts. "I love that you don't wear underwear," he says with a chuckle. "I love that you're dripping wet and all I've done is this."

"It's because it's been a long time," I retort. His hand stills, and I realize I just gave something away. Quinn thinks I'm pregnant already. "For us."

"Have you been dreaming about me?"

Fuck yes, I have. "No."

"Tell me the truth," Quinn commands. "Is it me you wanted when you were with that man? Is it me you thought of when he was inside you?"

I can't answer. No matter what the hell he does, I have to keep my mouth shut. He thinks I've been with someone else, and it needs to stay that way. "Why don't you fuck me and we can find out?" I say as I move my hands against his bare chest.

Quinn smirks. "Oh, I'm going to, that's not even a question, but how many times I let you come is dependent on your answer."

I will not let this smug bastard win. He wants to know if I thought about him while I was with someone else? Too bad. "If you wanted to know the answers to your questions, then you should've been around. And how many times you make me come will determine whether you ever touch me again."

I throw my own gauntlet down. It's up to him if he picks it up.

He leans onto his knees. Towering over me. "Well, then I better get to work."

Quinn unties his shorts, watching me watch him, and then pulls them off, freeing his dick.

I am one of the few women who love a man's dick. There's something oddly sexy about it. How it grows, tastes, and moves. My body was made for him to fit inside me, and I am so going to enjoy this ride.

My hand reaches out to touch him, but he pushes it away. "You want to touch me?"

I nod.

"I thought I was the one who had to earn it?"

"Then what are you doing?"

His eyes fill with mischief and a hint of challenge. "It's only been you, Ashton," Quinn informs me and then wraps his hand around his cock. "I've been hard for you, wanting you and no one else. I don't give a fuck if you believe me or not because you're the only woman I want."

My breathing accelerates as I watch him stroke himself while looking at me. I'm jarring back and forth from anger to love. Each side gets the lead only to be dealt a losing blow. I can see that he's aware of what this is doing to me.

His words are penetrating the armor I thought I had around my heart.

I don't want to hear anything else. "I want my orgasm."

Quinn shakes his head, his hand stilling. "How badly?"

"Enough for me to go find my vibrator if you won't complete your task."

I'm not even joking. I'm about two seconds away from attempting to lock myself in my bedroom. I'm not naïve enough to think I'll actually get that far, but I'm not about idle threats.

His fingers tuck into the waistband of my shorts, and he

pulls down. He lifts my legs to remove them completely, and then his hands grip my thighs and the backs of my knees are on his shoulders.

Before I can make a noise, his tongue is against my clit. He takes a few slow swipes, and I start to climb. He moves in small circles, adding and adjusting the pressure according to the sounds I make. I try to fight it off as long as I can, but he's too damn good. Quinn knows my body and what I like, and he pushes me.

"Quinn," I start to call his name as a pant. "There! Yes!" I yell as he starts to increase the pressure. Then he inserts a finger, curving it, driving me higher until there's nowhere to go but over the edge. "Holy shit!"

He keeps going, milking every ounce of pleasure from me as I thrash my head back and forth.

"There's one, I'm thinking it's a threepeat kind of night," Quinn says as he climbs my body.

"Yeah?"

He thrusts into me in one motion, causing me to cry out. "Yeah, maybe even four."

Death by dick . . . what a way to go.

chapter eleven

ASHTON

*Q*UINN BRINGS MY BODY TO ALL THE HEIGHTS, AND NOW WE'RE both sweaty, sated, and I'm lying on his chest. So much for self-control.

Both of us have been silent, either afraid to speak or afraid to acknowledge what just happened. Having sex with Quinn was definitely not in my plans. In fact, it was the opposite of what I was going to do.

Now, it's done, and I'm left feeling things I would rather ignore. Like I love him. Too bad he thinks I'm pregnant with another man's baby and will probably lose his mind when it sets in. Sure, he says that he doesn't care, but I know him. He's a prideful bastard. I'll really be dead when he finds out I was lying all along.

I rest my chin on my hand, looking up at him. "Loving you has never been an issue, you know?"

His eyes fill with an emotion I can't place and wish I could read. "No." He sighs. "It's been mine. I wasn't the man you needed, and you're pushing me away now because I deserve that." With that confession, the emotion in the room shifts. "If I were a better man, I would do what you're asking. I'd leave and let you have the life you want—without me. But, you see, I've tried that for the last six months. I've lived in this world without talking to you, touching you, or knowing you were there, and I was miserable. I wished I had died that day in the accident because a life without you, Ashton, isn't worth shit."

I shift to sit, covering myself with the blanket as I take in what he said. My heart is breaking because I've felt the same in some ways. I've missed him desperately. Our love is infinite and there are no breaks, but even though that is a truth, it doesn't mean it's healthy. We have very real, very major issues.

"I'm sorry I tried to slap you. I never should've done that."

He takes my hand in his. "I'm not. I was out of line. Here I am, trying to prove that I've changed, and I hurt you so that you can't hurt me first."

"And here you are, doing what I've asked you to do for years, and I can't accept it."

Quinn's fingers tangle with mine as though, if he just holds on tight enough, we can't break apart. "I will do whatever it takes. I'm on leave for a month, and I'll take a month after that if I have to. I'm sor—"

This is not going to end well for me. I already know it. When he wants something, he gets it. I have to remember that sometimes when someone gets something they want, they also give it back.

"Don't," I say quickly. "Don't apologize. We're both at fault. I know you're hurting right now." My hand touches his chin, drawing his attention back to me. "Let me in. Tell me what happened and how you got injured and sent home early."

He seems to debate for a moment, and then his eyes close as he does what I ask. "We were in the Humvee, talking about King's upcoming wedding. He was fucking happy. He couldn't wait to get back home so that he could make Tessa his—not like she didn't own him already, but that's beside the point. Then it was like nothing. No Earth, no ground, no world around me. The laughter was gone, and it was replaced with deafening sounds."

I fight back the tears that form when I think of him and the fear that must've been in that vehicle. He takes my hand in his, holding it against his chest and lacing our fingers.

"I was watching it all happen, but there was no slow motion. It was so fast that I couldn't process anything. There was screaming, but I couldn't tell where it was coming from, blood was splattered on my face, and I had no idea if it was one of the guys' or mine. When the flipping finally stopped, I didn't want to focus. I wanted to pretend it didn't happen because the quiet was worse than the noise. Quiet means that people were dead."

I tighten my fingers, letting him know I'm here, but he doesn't respond. This had to be incredibly difficult to recount. I raise my other hand to his face, going very slowly and giving him time to escape. "I'm so sorry. I wish . . . I wish I could . . ." I don't know what I wish for because nothing will make it better. "I know how much those guys meant to you."

He nods, his eyes on mine but the anguish is hard to see. This man, this strong, fighter of a man, is breaking. "I was able to get everyone out, but we lost King. Of all the guys we lost, it shouldn't have been him. I was so upset, but then all I could fucking think about was you. You, Ashton. There, in the middle of me possibly dying, your face was the only thing I could focus on. The regrets that filled me were sitting on my chest, and all I could think about was getting back to you. So, don't fucking tell me I don't love you."

My lip trembles. "And then you get back and were met with my glowing reception."

He gives a half-smile, one that doesn't reach his eyes. "I don't expect this to be easy."

"No, it definitely won't be."

"I know that I have a lot of groveling to do."

"Yeah." I nod. "I'd say that."

"But I'm willing to do it. I'll fight through whatever line of men is trying to take my place. I'll slay any dragon if it means I get you in the end. I know talk is cheap and that I've made promises I couldn't keep before, but I want to give you whatever you want."

His fingers wipe away a tear I didn't feel fall. "I've only ever wanted you."

"You have me." His voice is soft.

"I mean all of you. I want a life, Quinn. That means you coming home to me, loving me, having a family. I don't want a relationship that is so confined that it's easy to walk away from. Regardless of how much you thought pushing me away would make losing you any easier—it didn't."

"I know. I know I can't give you everything you want, but I will do what I can. I will be a better man." He shifts, forcing me to sit up. "I need time to figure out how to do it, and I need you to help me."

I close my eyes and let another tear fall as an echo of a past promise whispers to me.

He'd asked that of me before.

Said almost those exact words.

What happens when he realizes it's not for him? I'm the one who is left stranded. That's what.

No. I said one time only and that's what this will be. A goodbye to the girl who believed Quinn would be her savior.

"There's no point, Quinn." I get up, pulling the blanket off the back of the couch and wrapping it around myself. "I'm going to have a baby, and we both know this won't work."

"How won't it?"

"Because I won't allow myself to hope for more. This never should've happened."

His head jerks back. "What shouldn't have happened?"

I point to the couch. "This! It was a one-time deal, and now I think it's time for you to go."

I don't want him to leave. I want him to stay, love me, give me everything, and yet, I know that's a fallacy I can't afford to hold on to. I've allowed Quinn to treat me the way he does. There was a precedence set that he could do what he wanted and I would stand by him. When I asked him to make concessions and he didn't, by not putting my foot down or walking away, I basically told him it was allowable. I've given him permission to break my heart so many times, and that is not going to end if I don't change.

Could things be different? Maybe.

Maybe he could end up being the best husband in the world, but based on the fight we had, I'm going to say it's not likely.

"So, that's it? You're going to give up? I already told you that I'll be here for you and the baby."

I scoff. "Please, you weren't even there for me when it was just me. How am I to believe that you'll stick around and help raise another man's child? How can you ask me to set myself up for that kind of letdown?"

He shakes his head. "No, I'll help raise your child, and that child will be mine. Just like you are."

I don't believe him at all. "Leave," I say with sadness.

"If that's what you want . . . then, fine, Ash. I won't keep fucking begging you to see that it's different this time."

If he were anyone else, I might have believed that. I wish so much that I could run to him, wrap him in my arms, and let him care for me. That isn't what we've ever been, which is heartbreaking. Our love has always been filled with contingencies. It's not the way I want to live anymore.

So, I shouldn't feel like someone is ripping my heart out right now. It shouldn't be hard to breathe as I watch him get to his feet and grab his clothes off the floor.

"I'm sorry it's like this," I say, and then my eyes drop to what's stolen his attention—the black book of baby daddies. I close my eyes and pray he doesn't realize what it is. He'll know I am . . . intentionally leading him to a false conclusion of my pregnancy, and then I'll really be in trouble.

His eyes meet mine. "Are you? Because, maybe you're right. I tell you that I've changed and then I show up here, fight with you, and we end up fucking on the couch. I'm sorry I keep doing this." Quinn pulls his shorts on and yanks his shirt back over his head. "I should go."

I turn and head to the window, not wanting to watch him leave me again. I stare out at the world that's moving on around me, ever-turning, changing, and I feel like I'm going in circles.

Quinn has been a part of my life that I never thought I would give up. There were happy times throughout the three years. Of course, we fight. That's who we are. He's an alpha asshole and I'm a stubborn bitch. However, when we are both just us . . . it is magical.

He made me smile, put up with me when I was crabby, and took care of me when I was sad. After the whole thing with my ex, Quinn never judged me. He didn't try to make me feel lower than I already felt. No, he stood there, horrified that any man would hurt two women so badly.

I think I fell in love with him that day.

Just that simply. As though there was really no other option. Loving him was inevitable, just like losing him was.

But he's here now, wanting another chance, and I slept with him. Does that mean anything?

"Look," I say with resignation after a few minutes of thinking. "Can you give me a bit of time to figure out my life?"

"I'll give you all the time you need to figure things out." He brings his lips to mine as his thumb rubs my cheek.

How can a short kiss leave me feeling so lost? I look away, wrapping the blanket tighter around myself. After a few minutes of me staring out at the glimmer of lights of the city, I hear him clear his throat. "I have to think," I explain.

"I know." He stands at the door, and I make my way toward him.

Once it closes, I need to lock him out of my apartment and my heart.

"It's a lot . . ."

He watches me, saying, "I know, and now you're going to have a baby, right?"

There is something about his tone that makes my senses spike. "Right . . ."

"I mean that there isn't just us to think about. You're going to have another man in our life and that'll mean compromise on both our parts."

My eyes narrow. "I don't think he'll be an issue . . . why are you being so understanding?"

"Me? I'm not. I'm stating the obvious. With you being pregnant and all . . . I need to think about the entire situation and how we could navigate the murky waters of co-parenting."

"Okay." He knows. He saw the book and figured it out and that's why his mood changed.

He turns, opening the door, and then stops in the hall before he's fully out. "You dropped this." Quinn hands me the black book. He leans in and kisses my cheek with a grin. "I'd pick the guy on page twenty. He looks the most like me."

Son of a bitch. "Which is why I haven't picked him."

Quinn smirks. "Also, you probably should've put the wine away before you opened the door."

"Asshole!" I close the door before he can reply, but I still hear his laughter on the other side.

Well, we'll see how hard he's laughing when he finds out I'm still going through with it.

chapter twelve

QUINN

*S*HE'S NOT PREGNANT. NOT YET AT LEAST.

It means I have time to change her mind about going through with this ridiculous plan to have a baby with some other guy. That's not happening . . . over my dead fucking body.

For the last few years, I've listened to her talk nonstop about a baby, which was part of the reason I walked away. Being a father was never high on my priorities list. I'm not opposed to kids. I love Liam's kids. I'm Uncle Quinn to Arabelle and Shane, and I spoil the shit out of them, but then I give them back.

I get to do all the things I'm not supposed to without having to deal with any of the consequences. Besides, having a kid would've gone directly against the plan to have nothing worth living for.

My alarm dings again, letting me know it's almost time to walk Ashton to work. I sit up and wince as the pain in my leg shoots through my hip. Last night, I overdid it. However, I'd take the pain a million times over again if it means having her in any way.

I stand and head to the bathroom so I can try to tend my

wounds. There's still a gash on my side that's red as hell today. As bad as this is, I was lucky and walked away with nothing permanent.

Bennett will need a shit ton of physical therapy, and Trevor was the worst of the three survivors. He's already had two surgeries to repair his leg, and I have no idea if he'll walk again. All we do know is that his time as a SEAL is over.

Which reminds me of a call I need to make.

Mark answers on the first ring. "Dude, you better have a good reason to call me this early."

"Good morning, Twilight," I say with a smile, knowing I woke him.

"Yeah, yeah. What's up, Quinn?"

I fill him in on the details of the accident and the fact that Trevor may need some help. His wife left him about a year ago, so he has no one, and when he gets discharged, he'll be totally fucked. When guys like us lose a part of what makes us who we are, we often don't recover. God knows that, if I wasn't able to do this, I'd be broken.

Being a SEAL isn't a job, it's who I am.

"I'll check on him. What about Bennett?" Mark asks.

"I haven't . . ."

"You haven't called?"

"I've been busy trying to get Ashton to forgive me." It's not an excuse, but if it were me in the hospital and him out here chasing his girl, he'd be doing what I am. He pretty much threw my ass out of there when I was released, demanding I go get her.

Mark chuckles. "I'm sure that's going well."

"It's a work in progress."

"Yeah?" Mark laughs harder. "I've known that woman for years, and she is stubborn as fuck."

I'm aware. "She'll come around."

"Right. Well, I'll reach out to Trevor and Bennett. You know that Jackson and I will do whatever we can to help any SEAL who needs a job."

"That's why I called."

Mark falls silent, and then, as if he can't help it, he starts in on me. "Listen, this call is great, but if you fuck with her head again, you're going to need to work with me too because I'll break both your legs. I know you're an idiot, and I've let that part go, but this last time you really hurt her."

Ashton and Mark have been friends since Catherine came around, and while I usually appreciate the whole big-brother thing, his threat is unnecessary. "I'm not going to hurt her."

"Good. See to it that you don't . . . that's if you can get her not to kill you first."

"I love her," I say to him because he understands. Mark was a lot like me in the way he felt about relationships. We had this talk when I first started dating her.

"Took you long enough to figure it out."

I laugh once. "Yeah, no shit. I have to start on part two of this, thanks for helping with the guys."

"Don't mention it. Good luck taming the feral cat." Mark hangs up while chuckling.

I feel like the biggest dickhead and hate that all my friends think the same thing. I don't know what the hell was wrong with me, but now that I'm aware of how badly I fucked up, I'm going to make it right.

No matter what I do, I'll put back her broken pieces and hold them together.

chapter thirteen

ASHTON

"ALL YOUR TESTS CAME BACK GREAT. I SEE NOTHING THAT should prevent you from being able to conceive," Clara says with a smile. "I'd like to try intrauterine insemination first, and if we're not successful with that, then we can explore other options."

My God, this could really happen. "I don't know what to say."

"Have you picked the donor?"

I shake my head. "I didn't look yesterday. I wanted to, but it was late, and well . . . someone took up my damn time. But I'll have all weekend."

Tonight, I'm going to head to New Jersey to avoid my stalker, who has established his camp in New York. He didn't appear at my door this morning or during my commute, which was both great and a little disappointing. I thought he would've popped up with his smug and very sexy smile.

I spent the entire time looking over my shoulder, wondering when he was going to rear his ugly face—well it's not actually ugly at all. My muscles were tight until I got in the building, but that was when the frustration sunk in. Why did I want to see him? Why did it matter if he wasn't around? I should be happy about it because that's what I want. Who cares if I won't have another angry fuck session? I don't want that anyway.

"Great. Once you get that narrowed down, we'll get you on the schedule and get the medications ordered. Since your period is due in about twelve days, you can take the shot right after your last day, or you can wait another month if you haven't picked a donor."

Hell no I'm not waiting. "I'll have a man figured out by Monday."

"I'm sure you'll pick someone wonderful, Ashton."

I don't know about that, but whoever it is, they're about to have a kid and not even know it. It's so surreal. I can't imagine knowing that I donated an egg that would eventually be a baby without my knowing.

"Yeah, I'm sure too."

"Are you okay?" she asks with furrowed brows.

"This is really going to happen? I mean, it's real, right? I'm going to be a mom?"

Clara nods with a grin. "I hope so. As you know, success rates vary, but financially this is the best first step. We'll run some bloodwork right before and go from there. But I have a good feeling about your chances. We know you can conceive already, and there are no abnormalities."

"Right. I mean, this is all good news."

Her eyes stay on mine. "You're nervous?"

"Yeah." I laugh. "It's one thing when it's sort of conceptual, but when you know it can be a reality, it becomes a lot more . . . real."

Clara gets up from her seat and comes around the desk to sit beside me. "I encourage you to talk to your family, Ash. Not only because their support will be great, but so that you're not alone through any of the possibilities. I know you're this strong woman, and I admire you for it, but the added hormones can mess with your head."

Any medication could have side effects, but hormones are probably worse. "I'll think about it," I tell her.

I know my mother would be supportive, after she lost her mind. My father, though, I don't know. Catherine and Gretchen already are happy for me, but they're not here. In terms of a local support system, I'm really alone.

My cousins are all over the state and raising their own families. It seems like a lot to ask them to be around.

"Please do, I'll be here, but I'm also your doctor, so I have to keep our friendship separate a bit."

"I appreciate it, Clara, I really do."

"I'm happy you trust me enough."

"There were no other options. You're the best, and you know it."

She squeezes my hand. "I'm only as good as my embryologist."

"Speaking of your embryologist, I should get back to the lab. We have a few retrievals today."

"Okay, I'll talk to you next week?"

I get to my feet. "Definitely, and then we'll make me a baby."

Once work is done, I get home, pack a bag, and get in the car to trek out to Jersey. My mother was over the moon delighted that I was coming. No doubt she's cooking and running my father ragged to get all my favorite things.

My mommy is the best.

I know that I can tell her all about my issues with Quinn and she'll understand. Yes, she loves him, but she loves me more. It's the traitor I call Dad who I need to work on.

On the way home, I look for Quinn again, but I don't see him. I knew this would be the outcome and this solidified it. Nothing has changed. He doesn't love me or want a family. He got what he wanted and now he's gone again.

I pull into my parents' driveway, park, and make my way up the porch steps.

"I'm here!" I say as I juggle four bags and try to open the screen door that never cooperates. Sure enough, the one bag slips off my shoulder, slapping me in the face as I bend to adjust the other ones. "Help! Anyone!"

I hear my father's laugh and then hands are pulling at the bags. "Ouch! Dad, wait!" I groan as I'm trying to move the opposite way.

"Stop fighting, and it wouldn't be stuck." I hear the voice that does *not* belong to my father say.

I look up, my hair in my face, but I don't need perfect vision to know who it is. "And then the cat came back . . ."

Quinn chuckles. "I never left."

"Ashton, get inside, the air is on!" my mother complains.

I push my hair back and there is the grin that has haunted me all day. The look on Quinn's face says it all—he got me.

I allowed myself to think he was gone, allowed my guard to drop just enough that seeing him sends a rush of emotions over me. I'm happy, sad, angry, hopeful, turned on, and want to slap him all at the same time.

"Your mom made pasta fagioli," he says with his hand extended.

"I can smell it."

He nods. "It's your favorite."

"I know that, thanks."

"You're welcome."

I snort. "That wasn't a real thanks."

"I know, but any form of gratitude you send my way, I'm going to take it."

"Well, that'll be the last one."

Quinn's smile grows. "We'll see, I'm a charming man and have set my sights on you."

Oh, please. "I'm a grown woman who has her sights on something else. Now, let me in before my mother rips my head off about the air."

He takes a step back, grabbing all four of my bags with an ease I hadn't been able to pull off, and we head into the kitchen. My dad sits with the paper and Mom is fussing with the pot on the stove.

"I didn't know you were hosting company," I say as I walk to my dad. I kiss his cheek, and he grunts.

"Quinn isn't company," Mom says as she stirs.

Right. He's the son they never had.

I walk to her, giving her a hello. She touches my cheek with a smile. "You look tired."

"It's a wonder I'm not depressed after I visit."

"Don't be fresh," she chides. "I was saying that you're working too hard."

"Actually, it's not work that kept me awake last night. Quinn was over late and let me know all the things he was feeling."

Dad puts the paper down, and I wait for him to lay into him. My father is conservative, and I know he wouldn't like the idea of a guy in my apartment late at night. "You were at her place late arguing?"

Quinn straightens his back just a little. "We were, sir. I went over to explain how I felt, which you had suggested—"

"Wait! You suggested?" I eye my father.

"Go on," he says to Quinn, ignoring me.

"I told her, but as you see, I did a bad job of it. We argued, but nothing serious, and then I gave her some space like she asked."

Oh, please. There was no space between us last night, and there sure as hell isn't any now. "Space? You're at my parents' house where I came just in case you didn't actually leave for Virginia! This isn't space, my friend. This is the opposite." Dad grunts once and then picks the paper back up. "Daddy! Are you serious? You're not going to throw him out? Tell him how insane he is for being here when I *clearly* don't want him to be?"

"Nope."

"I tried to get her to see how I feel about her," Quinn says as if he's saddened by my unwillingness to see things his way.

Nice to see he left out the part where he had me naked.

"I think you did a good job *rising* to that occasion." I make the offhanded sexual joke and wait.

Dad doesn't move, his voice carries over the paper. "Most men rise to the occasion when they're forced to."

It's by the grace of God that I don't burst out laughing.

Fine. They want Quinn here, they can have him. I have a perfectly wonderful apartment a state away where Quinn is not.

I give my mother a kiss on the cheek, not wanting to be rude to her and suffer her wrath, and then grab my bags.

"Where are you going?" my mother calls out when she sees what I'm doing.

"I'm going home."

"Ashton!"

"Ashton Caputo, you put those bags down right now," Daddy says with his deep timbre that still makes my stomach churn. Damn him and his big voice. "Now, I don't know what has you all fired up, but you will not be rude to anyone in my home."

I want to curse, scream, throw something at him so he wakes up and sees that I'm not in the wrong here. However, I do none of that. "Yes, Dad."

"I know that you and Quinn aren't together any longer, but he's here as a friend of mine."

"Fine," I say as I cross my arms over my chest. "But when he leaves, I hope you remember I'm your daughter and this is mutiny at its best."

He rolls his eyes. "There's the Irish like your mother."

"What?" Mom's head snaps to him.

"He said there's the girl I wish was like her mother," I cover for him.

Dad taps his finger across his nose, which is our sign. He started it when I was in grade school. Each time I was sad, he'd quickly bump it across and smile. I thought it was so funny that I started doing it back. Then it became something we did whenever we wanted to say something but couldn't around Mom. Whether it was thanks or I love you or watch it, it's all in his eyes.

That one was a thanks, kid.

"I bet he didn't, but very sweet of you to cover for him. Why don't you go put your bags in your room and then come back when you're able to manage a sweeter disposition?" Mom says as not just a suggestion but a requirement.

Only my family would invite in the man who broke my heart and then expect me to be nice. I swear, they love to torture me. I think this is payback for all the times I made them sick with worry.

I put my bags down, grab the black book of donors, and flop onto my bed. I came here with a purpose, and I'm not going to let some guy mess that up. I'm on a mission, damn it. It's time to find a daddy for my baby.

chapter fourteen

ASHTON

"**W**HAT ARE YOU DOING?" QUINN ASKS FROM RIGHT outside the door of my childhood bedroom.

"Shopping."

Like the rest of my parent's house, this room is stuck. There is still the *90210* poster on the wall, which I can't take down because . . . Dylan. On the other wall is LL Cool J with his thick, puckered lips blowing me a kiss that I reciprocated many times. That man is still sexy as fuck. The only thing that's different is she threw out my old comforter and replaced it with a plain white one with new sheets. Other than that, it's still 1999 in my bedroom.

Dinner has come and gone, and I've stayed up here in a show of self-torture. The scents of my mother's cooking filled the room, causing my stomach to grumble the entire time, but based on principle, I didn't eat. They want to feed Quinn and force me to stay here, then I'll starve.

He's still standing there, not taking the hint that I don't want to talk or see him since all he got was a one-word answer. I don't have to check, I can feel his presence as he silently watches me turn another page.

"You mean for the father of the kid you're having?"

"Yup." Flip again.

"Find anyone good?"

"I'm still shopping, aren't I?"

I keep flipping the pages, not seeing the faces, and then my bed sinks beside me as he sits.

There goes pretending.

The heavy sigh releases from my chest, and I finally move my eyes to him.

It would be so easy if I didn't think he was sexy.

I could go about my life, walk right by him without feeling anything, and live. But my traitorous heart is drawn to him.

"Your parents went to bed."

I glance over at the clock. It's already ten, and I'm so glad they called it a night. If they hadn't, I would have eaten my arm off. I was that hungry and that stubborn. "Awesome. So you're leaving?"

He shakes his head. "I'm not. I'm going to stay. Your parents didn't want me driving back to Brooklyn this late at night."

Of course they didn't. "Super." I roll my eyes and sit up. "Don't you have a job to go do? Saving the world from evilness and whatever else it is that makes you happy?"

"You make me happy."

Here we freaking go again. I'm not taking the bait this time. I'm too hungry, and I might end up biting him. "Look, just go back to Virginia. Go be a badass, and we can part as friends, okay?"

"No, I don't think that's how this will go."

"Well, now I understand why they say you have a God complex. You don't get to make that choice."

Quinn chuckles and shrugs. "Maybe not, but I've been thinking that, since I only have six months left on my enlistment, I would start to explore my options."

"Please, God, make this stop."

"You didn't say that the other night."

I drop the book and glare at him. "I wouldn't talk too loudly here, the walls are paper thin, then again, maybe we should"— my voice raises—"discuss how we had sex."

Quinn shifts forward, his hand covers my mouth. "Are you trying to get me killed?"

I mumble, but his hand blocks the words. When he removes it, I grin. "Is it working?"

"You know, I'm not sure your dad wouldn't be happy about it."

I'm not either.

"Well, if you could leave me to finish my task . . ."

"Ashton," Quinn says my name while tucking his finger under my chin, "we should talk about last night and how you lied about being pregnant."

We should, but I don't want to. I'm still petulant enough to be angry about it all. "I don't have anything to say."

He laughs. "I doubt that."

I actually have a lot to say, but I don't think any of it matters. My heart is already so torn apart and struggling to find a way through it. I love him, and yet, it changes nothing. I'm still going through with the procedure and going to live my life. My having sex with him does not change anything.

"What's the point?"

His thumb brushes against my lip. "The point is that what happened between us matters. Do you not see how much I care? That even when I thought you were already pregnant, it was irrelevant regarding my feelings?"

That part is great. It's nice to see that he cares, but there's no way that he's going to sit idly by and actually watch me do it. "And what about now, Quinn? What about when I tell you that next week I'll be starting my process? Are you going to hold my hand through it? Because I don't think you will. You are not getting the picture that I'm done with us. I'm moving on, and I came here to tell my parents that I'm having a baby." I say the words as my hand hits the black book.

He looks down where the information is laid out. "Who's the lucky guy?"

"You want to know? I'll show you."

He grins. "Sure, let's look."

I fucking hate it when my plan backfires. I grab the book and flip to the page of the only guy that I put a sticky note on. It's not even like I can pretend otherwise because his all-knowing eyes have probably already seen it.

"This one."

He pulls the book onto his lap, and I feel sick to my stomach. This is the worst because, of all the damn candidates, he's going to know why I chose this one.

He starts to read aloud. "Thirty-six years old, green eyes, black hair, has a master's in business after completing eight years in the—" He stops.

Our eyes meet, and I stand my ground. "Please, go on."

Quinn doesn't miss a beat. "Navy with six years as a navy SEAL."

"I found your replacement," I say with smugness. "Or maybe it even *is* you since there's such an uncanny resemblance to your life."

He closes the black book and hands it back to me. "Or you could pick me."

Oh, please.

"Pick you? Why the hell would I pick you when I've already had you, and clearly, it didn't work out?"

"No, but that was then, and I'm here now. I'll happily give you a few squirts."

"Gross."

Like I would want to have a baby with him. No thank you. I have enough drama in my life, and I don't need to have a mini Quinn around.

Or at least that's what I'm lying to myself about.

The truth is, I've wanted that for a long time. How dare he come in now and offer?

"You've got some nerve," I say with anger pulsing through me. "You come back after years of playing with my heart and offer to be my donor? Screw you."

"We've already done that. I'm happy to do it again."

I roll my eyes. "It wasn't that good."

Quinn tenses, and I hope I pissed him off. "I'm going to ignore that."

"Ignore away. I'm going to sit here and hope that your lack of sexual gratification upsets you enough that you leave."

We both know I'm full of shit, but wound me and I'm going to come for blood too. If he wanted to be the father of my child, he had all the time in the world to get it together.

"Regardless, we both know it's what we want."

Oh, please. "You're so full of shit."

He shrugs and moves in even closer. "Maybe I am."

"I know you are. You don't want a kid. You don't really want to be here for me. You want me back, and you're going to say whatever crap you can to make me think things are different. No need to be accommodating now, Ladykiller."

"I have two choices, *fragolina*. I can love you and let you make these choices because it's what you want or I can be a dick, and we both know that only makes you want something more. I'm picking the first."

"How pragmatic and self-centered. You think this is about you, but there is your first mistake. My having a baby has nothing to do with you. It's about *me*. I want this. I want to be a mother and start my family. I wasted forty-three-plus eggs on you, buddy, and I'm not wasting one single more."

He runs his finger along my cheek. "I see that, which is why . . ." He drops his hand and gets to his feet. "I'm here to make sure that nothing happens to you or the baby you'll be having with replacement me since you clearly don't want me."

"I need protection from you."

"Why is that?"

Because I still love you. Because you're in my damn head, and even with all the men in that book, I picked you anyway.

I bite my lips to keep from saying that. I can't make any mistakes—or any more than I've already made. I get to my feet, staring him down so we're on the same level. "You know what? You aren't going to change my mind, Quinn Miller. You're irrelevant to me and my life. If you want to follow me around, watch me get pregnant and round with another man's baby . . . that's on you."

His eyes flash with a hint of anger, and I fight back my grin. Yeah, he's not so okay with that, after all. It has to be killing him because, no matter what we say, we both belong to each other. I can't imagine the rage I would feel if I knew another woman was having his kid. I would lose my damn shit.

"We'll see."

I cross my arms and jut my hip out. "What? You think I'm not going to do it?"

"No. I know you will, and I'll be right there, holding your hand through it all. Pushing me away might be your goal, but . . . like I said . . . I'm here. You're stubborn, I'll give you that, but I'm not budging. So, do your worst."

Challenging me was a mistake. I take two steps closer to him, so we're nose to nose. "Oh, I will, but make no mistake, darling, my worst is just as bad as yours."

He laughs once and then wraps his arm around me, hoisting me to his chest. I squirm and try to fight back. "Put me down you idiot."

"I saw a spider."

I look around, wrapping my arms around his neck. "What? Where?"

"It was right there." His voice drops lower. "I saved you again."

There wasn't a spider, and I should be letting him go. I should be fighting, but I don't seem to want to. "Quinn . . ."

"Ashton?"

My pulse spikes, and my throat goes dry. I want to kiss him. Fighting with him is like foreplay, and I'm more turned on than I would like to admit. I could ask him, and I know he'd do it, but I pull on every last ounce of restraint I have. "Protectors don't typically kiss their charges."

His eyes drop to my lips. "Then we'll start tomorrow. Tonight, I'm going to kiss you, so call me whatever you want."

And, then, I no longer think about food because the only thing I'm hungry for is him.

chapter fifteen

ASHTON

"WHERE IS QUINN?" MOM ASKS AS WE'RE SITTING AT THE table.

"Hopefully, he's running his way back home."

She scoffs. "I hope not because your father is supposed to be with him."

It's just us this morning, my father and Quinn went for a run, apparently, he's healed enough to need to show off to my father. On a freaking run. My fifty-seven-year-old father, who hasn't run since he got out of the army, decided to do some good ole fashion PT with my navy SEAL ex-boyfriend. Like that doesn't have disaster spelled across it with a capital D.

"You know Dad is probably going to have a heart attack today?"

She shakes her head. "He'll be fine. He's as strong as an ox."

"He's also as big as one."

She laughs. "That's how you keep a man, my darling. You feed him."

"Then Daddy isn't going anywhere."

"Anyway, back to you and Quinn. Did you two talk last night?"

We talked and then we kissed. We kissed with so much passion that I was afraid I might die, but, man, I would've been okay with that as my exit plan. After his lips left mine, I pushed him away, remembering all the reasons it was a bad idea to be making out with him. He keeps getting the wrong impression.

I nod. "Sure."

"Well, that doesn't sound too promising."

"It's not. Now, when will Dad be back? I have some things to discuss with you both."

Mom leans back in her chair. "I was trying to talk about Quinn."

"Yes, and I was trying to avoid it."

My mother pushes the plate of bagels closer. "Eat, and whenever your father gets back, we can talk more about our ideas."

"I had one bagel already, Ma. I'm fine. But what do you mean your ideas?"

She shrugs. "It's just a few things that Quinn mentioned and we think he has a good plan."

I swear this woman is going to drive me to drink with her constant pushing. I know she wants me to be happy, and to her, that means marriage, but seriously, it's not going to work with Quinn. You'd think by now, they'd know that I'm the last person to do this with. The harder she shoves me toward Quinn, the faster I'm going to run the other way. I'm built that way.

Then again, maybe this is the best thing they can do.

"Listen, Mom, I do have something I want to talk to you about before the guys get here . . ."

There's no time like the present to get it out there. Not to mention it would finally get her to stop talking to me about *him*.

"Okay, sweetheart, what is it?"

"I'm going to have a baby."

"What?" she screams and then breaks off into prayer. "Oh, Lord, please forgive my daughter for her sins. Please understand that we tried to raise her right, but this is all from my husband's side."

"Mom!" I call to her as I place my hand on her arm. "Stop. I'm not pregnant, I'm just telling you what my plans are."

"You're not pregnant?"

"No, but I'm going to get myself pregnant. I'm going to go through the clinic to have a baby."

"Why would you do this? I don't understand. What about Quinn? What about a husband? You're going to just artificially stick it inside you?"

Oh my mother is so dense and yet so adorable. "I mean that I'm going to skip the husband and dating part and try to get pregnant on my own."

"Ashton, honey." She laughs softly. "You need a husband to have a baby."

"No, Mom. I need a man. I don't need to be married to him."

She makes a cross sign and closes her eyes. "This is too much."

I need to get her to see that there's more to this. It's about our family history not exactly being on my side. My hope is that she'll understand at least that part. "Do you remember what you went through to have me?"

Her eyes lift to mine. "Of course I do."

"And you remember how hard it was?"

"Ashton . . ."

"Understand that there are studies showing the fertility risks can be genetic. I have no idea why it was so hard or how you ever endured the number of miscarriages you did, not to mention the stress you put on your body to actually have me. It's truly just a small testament to the mother you are. I might have the same complications. The older I get, the more issues I might face, and I can't risk never being able to have a child. It would kill me, Ma."

She shakes her head, but there's a thread of understanding there. She lived it and somehow survived the suffering because, in the end, she got me. If I wait, I may not get the desired outcome.

"I don't want you to be alone."

I touch her hand, squeezing lightly. "I'm never alone. I always have you and Daddy."

"Yes, but you know what I mean, sweetheart."

It must be hard for her to see me this way. Her views are very old fashioned, and I am the furthest thing from that. I couldn't care less about having a husband before the baby. In fact, it would probably be more fitting for me to go the other way. At least then I would have a man who knowingly loved my child and me from the start, unlike if it were Quinn who never wanted kids.

"If I found someone—someone worthy and who loved me like I need to be loved," I tack on for emphasis. "I would've married him and be doing this the way you want me to, but I haven't, so I'm looking at my other options. I don't want to wait."

"I will always support you, Ash. You're the miracle that God granted me. I can only pray you'll wait and have a baby with a man you love, even if it's harder for you."

Her version of support and mine are a little different. "I'm not waiting."

"I figured. Well, then, I will pray that God gives you the baby you want and watches over you during your struggles."

Here's why I love my mother. Because even though she truly doesn't like any of it, she loves me enough to find a way through it. "Thanks, Mom."

"But you're going to do something for me."

And then I remember that her love sometimes also can be my biggest downfall. "I am?"

"Yes, you're going to be kind and considerate to Quinn."

Oh, dear God. She has to be kidding. "This is your one request? This is what you want me to do in order for you to be okay with me having a kid?" She shrugs as if it makes total sense. Maybe to her it does, but I don't get it. "Why is Quinn so important to you?"

"He's not, my darling girl, you are, and he loves you. Plus . . ." She sighs as she stands, gathering the plates. "We know that he'll stop this craziness and hopefully, in a few months, you'll be married to him."

There aren't words that seem adequate enough. I don't know if I could even attempt a conversation at this point. Still, I open my mouth before closing it twice. "You and Dad are nuts, you know that?"

"We're not the ones who are getting ourselves pregnant when there's a very nice man who would give anything to get another chance right in front of us. Who is the crazy one now, Ash?"

Her. It's definitely her. I'm smart enough not to say that because she's near the wooden spoon.

"You're right, Mom. I'm glad you love me and all my crazy."

She smiles and then touches my face. "Always."

Well, at least one parent is sort of on board, the other is easy because he'll never go against my mother. Now, I need to tell Clara my choice, and get this show on the road.

chapter sixteen

ASHTON

"GOOD MORNING," QUINN SAYS, STANDING OUTSIDE MY apartment door with a cup of coffee in his hand.

"What is this?"

"I thought maybe we should talk, but you've ignored my request sent via email, then two texts, and me at the door."

"And here I thought the ignoring of all that was an indication of what I thought of your request to walk me to work." I take the coffee from him and drink. If he's going to be persistent, he can suck it up that I'm going to be a terrible person to be around.

"Sure, you can have that."

"Thanks. I have a busy day today, and I appreciate you getting me the fuel to get through it."

Quinn nods with a smile. "I'll be sure to have one for you tomorrow as well. And the next day. And the day after that, and so on . . ."

"That's a lot of days and a terrible way to spend your income, but . . . I'm sure you'll figure it out. You can also bring me lunch. There's this awesome little pizza place on fifty-fifth that's like an orgasm in your mouth."

"I'll give you an orgasm in your mouth," Quinn says almost as a reflex.

"Been there. Done that. No thanks." I take a drink to hide my blush because that's exactly what I'd like to do.

God that man's penis is like a gift from the heavens. I'm going to miss it.

Hell, I'll miss sex.

I would've at least liked getting another good lay before the baby. However, I'm going to get knocked up, sans the big o. Although I did get quite a few from Quinn the other night, so they'll just have to tide me over.

I spent last night solidifying that man number twenty was, in fact, the best option. His physicality is definitely what I would be attracted to, not to mention he's smart, which bodes well. He's the kind of guy I could see myself dating and settling down with. I could've picked guy number forty-four who is a space engineer and holds two doctorates, but that doesn't sound like someone I would want to procreate with. So, normal and athletic is my choice.

Looking at the very nice specimen in front of me, I almost wish I could have sex with him again and not get attached. But that's not likely. I'm too damn emotional when it comes to him.

Quinn takes back the coffee and drains it.

"Hey!" I protest.

"If you're not going to be nice, you don't get your caffeine in the morning."

Bastard.

"You're fired from protecting me or being around me—again."

"Keep trying, *fragolina*. I'm unfireable." He grins. "Besides, I love you, and as the man who is willing to lay down his life for you, it's my duty to be here day in and day out until you see the error of your ways."

Seriously, this is going to be hell. He has no intention of giving up.

"Well, try to keep up," I say and then head for the stairs. I don't care that I'm on the eighteenth floor, that his leg hurts thanks to overdoing it with his stupid jog with my father, or that I can probably outrun him.

Going down the stairs is faster than waiting for the elevator.

"You think this is going to deter me?" he asks, staying right on my heels.

I knew it wouldn't, but at this point, making him miserable is my only source of entertainment regarding this entire situation.

Instead of arguing with him, which would probably end in some sort of kiss or loss of clothes in the stairwell, I put my music on and head to work.

Quinn does exactly what he promised when we were at my place, he is sort of there, but not. This time, there is no talking, taking my headphones, or irritating me. I'm able to get on the subway, get off, and grab my bagel and coffee from my favorite shop on the way, all without him even being in my line of vision.

I know he's there. Regardless of whether I can see him, I can sense him.

After I get my food, I walk the streets of Manhattan, smelling the roasted nuts, coffee, and smog as I go. All the while knowing that, if there's any chance of danger, he'll be right there.

When I'm about a block away, I decide to test my theory.

I push forward a little too hard, bumping a rather large gentleman dressed in a huge sweatshirt and a pair of jeans that are low enough to show that he's wearing Calvin Klein boxers. The force of my accidental bump sends his food and coffee tumbling to the ground. He turns, and in typical New York fashion, he yells. "Jesus! Watch where you're going."

"You watch it," I spit back.

"Lady, you pushed me, and now I'm out of my breakfast."

"Oh?" I sneer. "I'm so sorry you're so delicate that you can't handle it. Looks to me like you could afford to skip a few meals."

He glares, and I know this is going to be bad. "Excuse me?" The bald man takes a step toward me. "You push me and then you come at me like this? You should be apologizing or offering to buy me a coffee and donut, but you want to be a bitch? Fuck you, lady."

What started as a fun experiment has now pissed me the hell off. There are only four people in the world who can call me a bitch, and this douchebag isn't one of them. "Excuse me? You're calling me a bitch?" My Jersey accent gets even thicker. "Fuck you harder."

The bald asshole chuckles once. "You're not worth it. Stupid bitch."

I go to move forward to push him or maybe knock his ass out when a pair of arms wrap around me from behind, spinning me around before setting me down. I go to move, but I'm met with a very large and angry person blocking me with an arm out.

"Apologize to the lady," Quinn's voice is filled with danger.

The hairs on my arms rise as goose bumps appear.

Oh, you're in big trouble now, Baldy. My ex-boyfriend-navy-SEAL-who-can-kill-you is about to go commando on your ass.

I peek out from behind him with a grin. "You heard the man. Apologize or get knocked out."

Quinn levels me with a stare.

I slink back behind him, my hands on his broad back, and I can't stop smiling. He was here, ready to save me even if I provoked it. There's no doubt he knows exactly what I was doing, but then again, it serves him right.

"Look, I don't know who you people think you are, but I'm not apologizing to no one. She pushed me and then wanted to get tough, control your woman."

Oh, he's going to die. Maybe my big plan wasn't exactly the best idea. I touch Quinn's shoulder, squeezing gently. "Quinn, why don't we let Mr. Clean here go about his day with his shitty attitude."

He doesn't move.

This is bad.

I try again. "You know, you could kill him, but then you'd be in jail and I would be out in this big scary world without a protector. Imagine all the trouble I could get into . . ."

Not like I don't live a perfectly safe life pretty much daily, but whatever. He needs to calm down. Also, I feel a little guilty since I created this hot mess.

Quinn's shoulders relax slightly, and I use that opening to get around him. "Listen, you should go before he kills you, and he really will, we'll chalk this up to another day in New York City, okay?"

"Whatever." He huffs and then walks off.

Thank God.

I turn to Quinn, who is still fuming, and the small amount of guilt I had is now quite a bit more. I was trying to prove something to myself, but what if he hadn't been there? Then what? I would've been in some real trouble. Not to mention, I was toying with him, which is what I've accused him of doing for years.

"Thanks for jumping in like that," I say sheepishly.

Quinn closes his eyes, his hands holding my wrists. "Why did you do that?"

"Do what?"

"Ashton." His voice is full of warning.

This is even worse because he knows I did it to provoke him.

Damn it. "Because I was feeling bitchy. I don't want you following me around. I don't want to know you're there but not be able to see you. I don't want to feel any of these things."

"Feel what things?"

Oh, no. We're not doing this. "I have to go to work."

"You can't have it both ways. You can't want me to be there and not see me at the same time as you want to see me but not want me around."

"You're the one who came back and told me you love me," I say the last word in air quotes.

"I want to show you that I'm not the same man who deployed six months ago. What I went through over there, it changed me. I just need you to give me a chance. Let me show you that I love you, Ashton. Let me prove it."

All the fight drains out of me. Why does he have to say things like this? Why now when I finally have a plan?

"I . . . I need to go to work, Quinn. I have to think, and I . . . I don't know that I can put myself out there again. I don't know if I can relinquish my plans again only to end up alone."

His blue eyes fill with disappointment. "I understand. I'll be here when you're done. I'll be here until you can trust me again."

I turn and walk toward my building, hating this day.

Broken trust is a long and hard road to repair. There are obstacles and hairline fractures that we don't always see, and I worry that if we travel down that way, a patch will give out, sending us into the ditch.

chapter seventeen

ASHTON

AFTER THE DAY ON THE STREET, I HAVEN'T SEEN QUINN once. It's been seven days of me moping around, looking for him, and trying to play Where's Waldo, but coming up with nothing. This is what I wanted, but yet I feel broken.

Even with my best friend here to take me to my appointment, I'm miserable.

"What's wrong? Today should be a happy day!" Gretchen says as she nudges me. "You're going to get the medicine and give Clara your choice. It's a big day, Ash and number twenty is a lucky guy. Be happy."

"I should be, but . . ."

"But you miss Quinn?"

"Shut up."

She laughs. "Look, you guys have a long history, and it's normal to miss him."

"It's been a week. And almost three weeks of him being around all the time, now he's invisible. . ." Her eyes cast down and toward the side. What is with my friends and their withholding of information. Jesus. "What are you not telling me?"

"I'm not supposed to tell you if I'm clearly holding back." Gretchen trips over the words.

"Well, too bad."

She starts to fidget. "Fine, he's in Virginia Beach, which is why I came a week earlier. Apparently, you're not supposed to be alone so . . . yeah."

He left? He left and didn't tell me? What the hell is that? And then, he sends my best friend to babysit me. This is ridiculous.

And then my brain starts to function and I put together why he would leave on today of all days. "He knows what is happening today doesn't he? That's why he suddenly had to go to Virginia?"

"No, actually, he doesn't. Or at least, I don't think he does. He's meeting with some navy people or something. It was all official business, but if he does know . . ." She trails off, seeming to come to the same distinction I did.

"Yeah. It would make sense."

"Well, we can't change him, we can only talk about you and how you could be pregnant in a few weeks."

I nod. "Yeah, it's everything I wanted."

Gretchen looks at me and then releases a soft sigh. "It doesn't sound very convincing."

"It's fine."

"Okay, if you say so, but you're lying and we both know it."

I seem to be doing a lot of that lately, mostly to myself. I know this is what I want, but I wanted it *with* someone. No one plans to live out their life like this. Most girls dream of the man, not just the baby. I know I did.

It was just the wrong guy in the dream.

Facing that reality today is the saddest part.

Gretchen hooks her arm around mine as we walk into the clinic. "Well, I am happy for you. Cat really wishes she could be here too."

"Oh, that would've been a fun day. The three of us together as I find out when I can get knocked up."

She laughs. "Of all of us, the most likely to be involved in a threesome is you."

The sad part is that she's not wrong. "I love you both but not that much."

"Oh, please. You've tried to kiss me once."

I burst out in a fit of giggles. Leave it to Gretchen to make me feel better. "I was drunk."

"I know, but you laughed."

I rest my head on her shoulder. "Thank you for being here."

"Always."

And that's the thing about my life. I may not have the man that I thought I would, but I have friends and family that others would kill for. It makes this bittersweet moment not so hard to deal with, and I know that I'm going to be fine. I also know that, in time, I'll find what I want . . . even if that man isn't going to be Quinn.

"You're pregnant," Clara says with her hand over the file.

"I'm sorry, but we didn't even get to that part yet," I say, looking from her to Gretchen and then back to Clara.

"Yes, but the tests that we ran shows us that you're pregnant."

"I can't be pregnant, Clara, I didn't even have the IUI yet. That doesn't make any sense!"

Gretchen covers her mouth. "*Oh*, but you did have the sex, my friend."

Oh my God. I had sex. I had sex with Quinn almost three weeks ago. I don't even remember if we used a condom. No, we did. Right? We had to. I mean, we haven't used them in years because I was on the pill and . . . and I never told him I came off it.

I came off the fucking pill a few months ago when I wasn't having sex and started to form this plan.

I came off the pill, and then I had sex with Quinn and didn't even think . . .

"This can't be," I say quickly. "This is a false positive or something crazy with the system. The lab fucked it up!"

Clara squares her shoulders. "We both know the likelihood of that is low. I know you're emotional and that this is a shock, but you are pregnant. When your urine showed a very, very faint sign, we did the blood test and you are one hundred percent pregnant."

"Run it again!" I yell as I get to my feet.

This can't be happening. I know I wanted a baby with the doppelgänger of Quinn, but I didn't want this. I mean, it's a baby, which was the end goal, but not with him. Not when we're both so emotionally fucked we could write a book about it.

One stupid time, and here I am, knocked up with his baby.

"Ashy . . ." Gretchen's voice is calming. "I know you're a bit . . . umm . . . taken aback, honey, but Clara has the test results." She turns to Clara. "Can you show them to her?"

Yes, I work in facts and results. I need to see them so I can see where the lab screwed up, and when I do, I will go and personally fire the idiot who did it. Then we will be back on track, and I can have number twenty's baby and be just fine.

She hands over the lab work, and I sink into the chair. It shows blood HCG levels indicating a pregnancy.

I'm pregnant.

"This wasn't supposed to happen like this," I mutter.

"I know, but it's okay. You're pregnant, Ash. That's what you wanted, and I know it's not the way you thought it would go, but at least it's with someone you love."

No, that's what makes it worse. Now, I'll always have a piece of Quinn, so even when he's gone, which he is now, I'll never be rid of him.

My heart sinks as despair washes over me. Tears start to fall as I look at my best friend. "Someone who will never love me back."

"No, that's not true, and you know it. He's misguided, for sure, but he loves you."

"Yeah, he has a funny way of showing it."

Gretchen giggles. "Yeah, he got you a baby . . . that you didn't even want with him. Best gift ever."

I laugh without any humor. "We'll see just how much of a gift he thinks it is."

I hope he realizes there are no returns available on this one.

"What do you want to do tonight?" Gretchen asks as we're snuggled on the couch.

Yesterday, I didn't want to do a damn thing. I kept thinking about the little baby in my belly and how the hell I was going to tell Quinn about it.

It doesn't feel like wrapping a "World's Best Dad" hat is the best idea. I could just blurt it out and see how that goes or I could not tell him and lead him to believe that instead of getting the meds today, I got pregnant.

He would never know.

But I would, and there's no way I could ever honestly do that.

"Who cares?"

She tosses a pillow at my head. "Knock it off. I haven't seen you in how long? The least you could do is entertain me a bit."

I flip her off. "Entertain this."

"Can we at least call Catherine and tell her? That'll at least be entertaining."

"No."

I'm not telling anyone, least of all her. She'll tell Jackson, who will tell Mark, who will tell Natalie, who will tell Liam. Then, just like that, Quinn will know. Nope. We're not even going down the rabbit hole of talking to anyone.

"I don't want to sit in here and watch you mope. Let's go see a movie or grab some food? We could always walk around the city and people watch . . ."

I don't want to do any of that. I want to forget that this is happening and move on with my damn life.

"We should go dancing!" I say.

While we may not be the spring chickens we once were, Gretchen and I are going to attempt to stay awake past ten tonight.

"Dancing? You didn't want to do anything a minute ago, and now you want to get dressed and go dancing?"

"Yes. That is what I want. I want to hang out with my best friend and not think about babies, exes, or lists. I want to put on too much makeup and not enough clothes and stay out late, before nothing fits me. We can make this part one of your bachelorette party."

She eyes me suspiciously, but I know she'll never resist the lure of dancing. Gretchen loves the clubs more than I ever did. Ben doesn't dance, which she's totally okay with, but I know she misses it.

Besides, once I get big, I won't want to dance, so this is as good of a time as any.

"Sounds like a plan to me! God, I've missed this city." Gretchen sighs.

"I've missed you," I say feeling emotional.

"Aww. Aren't you becoming a big mush?"

"Whatever."

"Why don't you come to Virginia Beach for a week? Maybe after you tell Quinn that you're going to have his baby and he dies, you can swing by his funeral before we hang out."

My God, she's insane. "I can't with you."

"I'm just saying, he's going to lose it."

"I know, but a funeral?"

Gretchen shrugs without apology. "I'm low on creativity lately."

"It's all that sweaty sex with Ben. Got your head slammed on the headboard a few too many times."

"That man lives up to his call sign in all aspects of his life. He's rather . . . large and . . . enthusiastic."

I sit on the edge of the bed with a smile. "Now, this I want to hear . . ."

"Why?"

"Because . . . it's sex with your hunky boyfriend."

She makes a gagging sound. "You need boundaries."

"That ship sailed about twenty years ago. It's so hard being around my ex, who tends to make my libido spike when I'm so much as in the same room as him."

Gretchen grabs two dresses holding them up. I point to the short black one on the left and she nods. "Now you can at least have sex with him whenever you want, right?"

"Umm no."

There will be no more sex. If he wants, there will be co-parenting to the best of my abilities, but he doesn't have to do anything. I was totally prepared to be a single parent, and this changes nothing.

At least, it won't if I can keep ignoring the fact that I love him and he loves me back—or says he does.

But, even still, I can't go there. I have to stand my ground, even more so now that there will be a child involved.

"That's stupid. Why wouldn't you bang his brains out?"

"Because that sort of negates my entire argument about how we're not getting back together . . ."

"No one said you had to forgive him."

Okay, I'm convinced that she's had some kind of body invasion. Gretchen is the pragmatic one. She's ruled by reason and consequences. Every damn time we discuss anything, she's so over analytical that, by the end, I give up. I'm the one that tells people to do the dumb stuff, and she's trying to steal my role. No.

"What the hell is wrong with you?"

"Me?"

"Yes, you!" I slap my hands against the bed. "You're never like this. You're actually advising me to fuck my ex? The same guy who broke my black heart. The same one who I actually shed tears over? I'm missing something."

"Did you think Harold ever loved me?"

Ugh. Not Harold again. He was using her, and she never saw it. No matter how many times we told her, she found some lame excuse to stay with him. I swear I had never seen Gretchen as a weak woman, not until Harold. He was her boss, he took advantage of the situation, and when she was finally going to leave him, he proposed, only to leave her at the altar. I hate Harold and his tiny dick.

"No. And you know that."

She nods as though I made her point. "Right . . ."

"Right?"

"Are you trying to be obtuse?"

"No. I'm not following you."

Gretchen gets to her feet and begins to pace. "You and

Catherine told me a million times—hell, Harold basically told me as well, but I didn't listen. In the end, I was the one who was hurt. I was so sure he loved me, like you're so sure Quinn doesn't love you."

She's nuts. This is nothing like that. I'm not purposely ignoring my friend's advice. They both see traits of the men they love in Quinn. Jackson would do anything for Catherine. He'd slay dragons with one arm behind his back. Ben would smash anyone who ever tried to make Gretchen feel small. They're failing to see that those guys are men while Quinn is a little boy.

"Gretchen, we were telling you because you were making a mistake. It wasn't because we did or didn't like him. That's the difference."

"Oh, of course, only you're right when it comes to this?"

I'm glad she sees that. "Pretty much."

"You're an idiot. Quinn loves you, and both Catherine and I see it. You're making the same mistake only in reverse. But you know what? That's on you."

"Is this what you came to New York for?" I ask. "To get me to change my mind?"

Her eyes widen, and her jaw falls slack. "No! I came here to help you pick your baby daddy, which you didn't actually need me for, and because Quinn asked me to come while he was away."

We'll get to that second part later because that makes no sense. I've lived in this city for years by myself, and there's no reason why anyone should be worried about me being alone. Ridiculous.

"Since it seems your mission is done, can we go out and enjoy our night without thinking or talking about Quinn?"

"Of course. I'm sorry."

"Don't be sorry, Gretch. This is what we do."

We're the friends who can say whatever it is that we truly think and then get over it and move on. Which is exactly what I want us to do. Fighting about this isn't going to change my mind.

"Well, let's have fun and dance the night away."

I smile and nod once. "That's what I'm talking about."

Now, let's see if I can actually accomplish it.

chapter eighteen

QUINN

"WHAT THE FUCK AM I DOING?" I ASK LIAM AS I SLAM MY hand onto the counter. "Why am I going back there?"

"I don't know. I guess you should stay here since it's not going your way, right?"

I'd really like to punch him in the face, but since I'm standing in his kitchen, that seems a bit rude. "Thanks for the advice."

"It's better than the shit you fed me when I was dating Lee."

I was so stupid then. I had this idea of what was right and wrong, and I was a shitty friend. He wasn't doing anything inappropriate, but there's a code we live by, and fucking another SEAL's wife—even if he was dead—was not okay. However, all anyone needed to do was spend a minute with them together to see they were right for each other.

Natalie made Liam a better man. Liam gave Natalie strength when she needed it.

Still, I didn't support my best friend, and for that, I'm still sorry. "I was a dick."

"You still are," he says with a laugh.

"Yeah, but I was wrong, and I'm sorry."

Liam sighs. "We've already had this out, dude. We're fine. You came running here when the unit returned from deployment, and I don't understand why. Other than you're lost and needed my expert advice because you probably fucked up your plan to wear her down."

And I guess I'm still stupid too.

I thought that Ashton would've seen the truth and come around. Sure, she kisses me like she can't help herself and we had some pretty fantastic sex, but then she always walks away. Her touching me is more of a reflex than a want, and I'd like it the other way around.

"None of it is working in a meaningful way."

"Well, let's recap your brilliance, shall we?" The sarcasm in his voice is not at all reassuring that he believes I'm at all brilliant. "First, you arrive at her parents' house without talking to her first and use your injury to get sympathy. Then, you rent a room in the same apartment building she lives in with the purpose of proving you're not going anywhere. Really smart." His tone is pissing me off. "But that's nothing compared to you following her around even when she's pretty much said in a hundred ways she doesn't want you there. Let me know if I missed any key points. Oh, wait, I forgot, you screwed her too—and not in a way that proves you love her."

Natalie walks into the room, rolling her eyes. "Don't give up, Quinn. Women love to be pursued!"

"See, your wife thinks it's a good idea."

"She didn't say that. She just said not to give up. We all know this is going down in a blaze of glory, which I'm assuming you know as well. I'm not sure how you think this plan of yours will work."

"That's not what I said." Her hand rests on Liam's shoulder. "I think it's admirable that you're going there. When I was dealing with my life falling apart, Liam was here. Showing up is what a woman wants. I know it feels worthless because nothing seems to be changing, but you have to put in the time."

No amount of time is going to work, and that's the scary part of it all. I'm not going to win her back because I've failed her too many times.

"And if time isn't enough?" I ask.

Natalie smiles softly. "Then you'll have to ask yourself if you did enough. Ashton has a huge heart, and no matter what she says, it belongs to you. She needs to find a way to trust you with it again."

I know she's right.

"So, what's your plan?" Liam asks as he takes a drag of his beer.

"I'm submitting early discharge papers tomorrow or a medical release and moving to New York."

The beer goes flying across the room and both of them stare at me. "You're what?" He practically yells his question.

"I'm getting out. She's more important than all of this. She wants a husband who isn't always leaving. She wants kids and a life that I can't give her while I'm still enlisted. Ashton has a great job there, I won't ask her to leave it."

Natalie opens her mouth and closes it. "Well, I'll be damned."

"Why are you two so shocked?"

"Are you fucking kidding me? You're the one who gave me shit when I talked about getting out. You said this life is all men like us know, and you've suddenly had a change of heart?"

I walk around the counter and sit across from him. Liam has been my best friend for more years than I care to count, and I've always had his back, just like he's had mine. There's a brotherhood in our line of work, but ours is even deeper than that. He's the guy that I never have to question. When he's on my six, I know I'm set. He explains it the same way.

No matter which way one person turns, the other has already anticipated that move. It seems I caught him off guard for the first time.

"And I believed that. I thought the team is what made me who I am, and now I see that's not the case."

"All it took was an IED to make you see it . . ."

I roll my eyes. "You about done being a dick?"

He shrugs. "Maybe. It's too easy when it comes to you."

Natalie slaps his arm. "Stop it. If this were me, what would you do to win me back?"

This should be good.

Liam releases a heavy sigh. "Everything. I would stop at nothing until I had you where you belong—with me."

Her eyes go soft. "Exactly. So, how about you stop giving him so much crap and actually help him out?"

I think I just fell in love with Natalie.

Liam goes quiet, and knowing him as well as I do, I know he's trying to find the words in the best way to tell me to give up. "Listen, man, I know you love her. I feel for you on a deep brotherhood level there. When you know that she's the girl for you, it's impossible to let that go. I think the way you're doing it isn't working. Getting out is a start, but . . . if we were in the trenches, what would you do? How would you get yourself out of the place you've pinned yourself?"

I think about it in a different way. If I were in a tactical situation and the enemy line was holding strong and there were no weaknesses, I'd adapt. There's always a way, it's finding the method of achieving success that is the tricky part.

"I need to change my plan."

"Yeah, that's a start."

"I need to prove it and not by pissing her off."

"Another good idea. One more, and we might have ourselves a miracle."

I ignore the asshole's comment. What can I do? What is it that she needs? "She wanted me to choose her, let her into my life. All she ever wanted was to matter."

He clears his throat and fake cries. "My little boy is growing up."

"Fuck off."

"I'm glad you're pulling your head out of your ass, Quinn. Now, figure out how to show her that, and you might just get your girl back."

Yeah, that's exactly what I'm going to do.

chapter nineteen

ASHTON

CALLED OUT OF WORK TODAY, WHICH IS A RARITY FOR ME, but I need a mental health day after Gretchen left last night. I'm still reeling from the news that I'm with child—Quinn's child—and decided sleeping in and trying to get my head together was necessary. Normally, I would head to Jersey and see my parents when trying to hide, but that didn't work out too well last time, so today, I'm going to embrace my city. It's been a long time since I've gotten to do any of the Manhattan type things.

Since my entire life is filled with the daily sightings that most people come here for, I tend to forget to stop and appreciate them.

I'm going to change that. Besides, the sunshine and fresh air might help me make sense of the muddled crap inside my brain.

I open the door to my apartment, and there is a huge vase filled with red roses. I lean down and grab the card.

Fragolina, Roses are red, just like your head. If you could forgive me, I'd take you to bed.

I burst out laughing. Only Quinn would freaking leave a card like that.

Adorable idiot, but still.

Once I bring the flowers inside, I grab my phone and send him a text. We should probably talk soon anyway.

Me: Thank you for the flowers and your offer for a repeat. I see you're back in town.
Quinn: I owe you a lot more than flowers. I'm here, but I'll keep my distance since that's what you want.

Oh, Quinn, you have no idea how much that is going to change.

I know I need to tell him, but I'm not ready. I haven't even grasped this entire thing. My head and my heart are at war, and soon enough, I know he and I will be as well.

Me: Okay. Well, thank you. Does this mean you're leaving again soon?
Quinn: No.

That makes no sense.

Me: I don't get it. If you're going to keep your distance, then what exactly are you doing in New York?
Quinn: Exactly what I came to do, win your heart again.

My initial response is to tell him to give it up and that it's never going to happen. Then there's this other part of me that whispers how much I love him and that I'm unable to resist him. There's a part of him that's growing inside of me making my heart soften toward him.

Had he never come back, I could've gone on with everything.

I would've had no issues navigating my decision to have a baby because, when we parted, that was it for me. Sure, I cried, hated him, went through all the stages of grief, but I was right at the beginning of acceptance.

But he did come back, and he got me pregnant, throwing all my plans to shit. What am I going to do now? I'll have to see him. There's no way Quinn will be an absentee father like his was. That man screwed with his head so much that he's still recovering from it.

He'll want to be a father to our child, but that doesn't mean that I have to let him back into my life, right?

Right.

I groan at the flowers. "Stupid boy!"

Instead of allowing this to fester, I choose to let it go and keep my plans to ignore him and pay attention to the rest of the world.

When I open the door this time, my plans are thwarted once again.

"I preferred the flowers," I say.

"I prefer you."

Quinn is there, unshaven with the scruff almost a beard, his hair is pushed to the side, and his smile is heartbreakingly beautiful. If his shirt weren't practically painted to his thick arms or his muscles weren't quite so defined, it would make it easier to ignore him.

Then my mind recalls the way he looked naked, and damn if I don't want to pull him inside and see about taking him to my bed instead of the couch.

"I was on my way out," I reply, hoping he'll take the hint that he's not required.

His eyes rake my body, taking in the sweatshirt dress and chucks I'm wearing. I wanted to be cute and comfortable for my outing.

"I see you called out of work."

"Not that it's any of your business . . ."

Quinn smirks. "No, it's not, and I wasn't judging. I missed you and wanted to talk."

My pulse spikes as fear hits me. What if he knows? What if Gretchen told Ben and he told Quinn? "Haven't we done enough talking?" I ask, hoping he'll reveal whatever it is he wants to discuss.

Quinn steps forward. "You see, I think that's the issue. We don't talk, as you once pointed out. We never really have. We were together for years, but in that time, I was gone and you were here. It got me thinking, why would you believe me when I've never told you how I feel?" I take a step back, wondering what the hell has gotten into him. "Then I came back, thinking I could explain to you I had changed, but when that didn't work, I forced you to be around me when you didn't want to be, which was dumb."

"Yes, that is all true."

He looks up, and the determination in his eyes stuns me. "I want to *prove* it, Ashton. I want to show you that I mean what I say by giving you what you need. I haven't done that."

"I think when we slept together it was a clear indication . . ."

"No." He shakes his head. "That night was the opposite of what I wanted to show you."

"I don't understand."

I thought the night we slept together was exactly what we do. We fight. We have sex. We mess everything up and then pretend it never happened. Only, this time, I won't be able to pretend. I walked away with more than just the proverbial T-shirt.

"I'm in love with you. So deeply in love with you that I don't think there will ever be a way out. I know you don't believe me, and I've done a pretty wonderful job of screwing up any chances to prove it, but that ends today. I don't want angry sex, well"—Quinn smirks—"that's a lie. I definitely want that, but not because you're trying to make me leave you. Things are going to be different for us."

"Really? How?"

Quinn takes another step forward. "I want us to date."

I stare at him, waiting for the punchline. "Didn't we do that for three years? Didn't pan out so well."

"We didn't date, Ash. Not seriously. So, I would like to know if you'd be willing to have dinner with me or lunch or breakfast or, hell, just a snack?"

"Are you seriously asking me on a date? Like a real date where you pick me up, pay, and I get all dressed up?"

Quinn nods. "Not very well, it seems."

In all the time we've been together, I don't think that's ever happened. When we started our relationship, there wasn't anything official. I was in Virginia Beach, we met, we were attracted to each other, and we slept together. Since it was really freaking good, we kept doing it. Then we were . . . a couple.

Dates were more of us hanging out and lots of fantastic sex.

But can I date him? I mean, we're going to have a baby. I don't know that it could ruin things any more than they already are. I love the stupid jerk. I'm already pregnant. What's the harm in dating?

There's always the risk of getting my hopes destroyed. Although, I don't have any hope that he's serious this time. So, that should take care of that.

"I'm not sure what to say . . ."

He smiles and takes another step forward, clasping my hand in his. "Ashton Caputo, will you go on a date with me?"

Butterflies take flight in my stomach, reminding me of how much Quinn can wreak havoc on my heart. Regardless, I would like us to find a way not to be enemies. It would make this less painful for both of us in the long run.

"How about we start with something a little easier?" I offer.

"Easier?"

"Yeah, I took off today since I didn't sleep much last night, so why don't you do some sightseeing with me? If that goes well and I don't throw you off the top of the Empire State Building, then we'll have dinner. We can . . . just . . . be friends first."

Quinn grins and brings my hand to his lips, pressing with the slightest pressure. "I can't wait for dinner."

So damn sure of himself. "I wouldn't put the cart before the horse, Ladykiller."

His eyes meet mine, and I see the mischief in them. "They call me that for a reason."

I snort. "Yeah, because after a day with you, most women want to kill themselves . . . or you."

The sound of his laughter is so freeing I can't help but smile. He pulls me into his arms, chest vibrating with the deep timbre of his amusement. "I guess we'll find out how it goes today."

I extricate myself from his embrace. "Yeah, I guess we will."

No matter how charming he is, I will not allow myself to enjoy it.

chapter twenty

QUINN

'VE VISITED ASHTON IN NEW YORK FOR A DAY OR TWO IN THE past, but we usually spent our time holed up in her apartment, making up for lost time. I've never gotten to see the city like this.

"And this is Times Square," she says as we stand in the center.

"It's seriously exactly like I always thought it would be."

"How's that?"

I look around, watching the billboards change every few seconds, people snapping photos, the looks of awe on peoples' faces as they are taking it in, and the crystal ball sitting there and reminding everyone that this is where the mark of the new year happens. "Just that it would be cool."

Ashton nods as she scans the crowds. "No matter what time of day, it's always like this. When it's dark out, it's amazing. The brightness of these few blocks is pretty nuts and you can't even begin to process it all because there's too much to look at. We'll have to make sure we come back at night sometime."

"I would like that," I answer.

She said *we* and *night*. I'm going to take that as a win. So far, I've done everything I could to keep it light and make her smile.

We have talked about what she wanted to see on the train and her very non-plan of a plan to maximize the day. The only thing I asked her to see was the Empire State Building.

My plan is to get her to Central Park, though. I got a tip from a friend of hers that it's her favorite place. She and Catherine used to go there around lunch and she swears there's magic there.

"Okay." There's a sense of unease in her voice.

"What about shopping on 42nd Street?" I change the subject, not wanting her to go in her head. God knows that's never a good thing. We've managed to keep all talk of us and a future completely out of our conversations. I think that's the best option if I have any hopes at dinner.

Her smile is wide. "Tiffany's is on 42nd."

I knew that was coming. Gretchen also happened to mention that a man in the dog house could always inch a little farther out with a certain blue box.

Hell, I'm so far inside that house I'll need several blue boxes to gain an inch out of it. "Do you want to go?"

Ashton's eyes narrow. "Do cows like to moo?"

"I'm not sure if they like it or if it's a reflex."

"You're an idiot."

"I know this. Do you want to go?"

She looks as though she's at war with herself, but I don't know that she can avoid the pull to shop. "Why do you want to go?"

I take a step closer. "We're on a trip to see all the things in the city, and isn't that part of it?"

"I hope you know what you're asking for," Ashton tells me as she runs her hand along my chest.

"All I'm asking is for you to enjoy the day."

"Well, if a trip to Tiffany's is in the cards, then you've secured that."

And then I'm going to take you to the park, and after that, I'm going to do whatever else I can to give you a day you never forget.

"Good. Lead the way," I say extending my arm.

We take the subway, and for the first time since I came back, Ashton seems relaxed around me. There are no seats and all the poles are taken, so I find a space and pull her against my chest, allowing her to use me as the pole. I stand, unmoving, hoping she sees that I want to be what holds her up. I don't want to tear her down or allow her to fall, but I'm not delusional enough to think her trust will happen without a fight.

Not with her.

She's going to make me work long and hard.

Once we reach our stop and exit the subway, the loss of her touch is all I can focus on. For those few minutes, I felt alive again. I take her hand and wrap it around my arm. She looks over, and her eyes dance to where her hand is resting. "What is this for?"

"I don't want you to get lost."

Ashton smirks with one of her classic eye rolls. "Right."

"You don't believe me?"

"I don't believe that's the reason you want me to hold on to you, but . . ."

"But you'll go with it?"

She shrugs. "For now."

We walk a bit and this side of the city is no less busy, but it's nothing like Times Square. People aren't snapping pictures like crazy, they're just moving around with bags from whatever stores they were in. It feels slightly calmer.

"Here we are," Ashton announces.

"So this is *the* Tiffany's?"

"The very one."

My plan was to let her pick out a few things, not giving a

shit about how much money it costs me because she's more than owed it, but now I want to be the one to choose. I want to show her that I know her. If she picks it out, then it's less meaningful.

"Do you want to go in?"

Ashton shrugs. "Do you?"

Fuck, I'm screwing this up already. "Come on, let's go look."

Her smile brightens, and she nods. "I've never gotten a box."

"Never?" I ask with a bit of smug pride building inside. I don't want any other man to give her things. I want to be the one who does these things from now on. She will have whatever firsts I can provide.

I want to ruin her for any other man or the idea that there could be another man, just like she's ruined me.

"You were tipped off!" She accuses as we enter Central Park.

"About what?"

"My love of this place, you sneaky asshole. You and my friends are dead to me."

Her friends aren't my only allies in this fight. I had a very long talk with her parents, explaining what my feelings and intentions are. She knows her dad is on my side, but she has no idea her mother has switched allegiances. While I may have won over the people in her life, I know I haven't come close to getting her there.

"Go easy on them, *fragolina*, I can be very persuasive."

Ashton huffs. "Yeah, I see that."

I move to take her hand, but she surprises me by doing it first. Her fingers wrap around my arm as we move through the park. "Are you getting hungry?" I ask.

"A little, but it's so nice out, so let's enjoy the warmth and fresh air for a bit."

"It's much better than the dungeons of your lab, isn't it?"

She laughs. "Yeah, it's a bit dark there, but I love what I do."

So much so that you're going to do it to yourself.

I stop myself because fighting with her is the last damn thing I want. I need to be patient. The fucking idea of her pregnant with another man's baby makes me absolutely out of my mind with rage, but I will not show my hand.

I lost that right when I let her walk out that door. At least that's what Liam, Natalie, Catherine, Gretchen, and Ben have reminded me of. Each one has not so subtly explained that pushing her is the biggest mistake I could make.

And that if she does this, it'll be something I have to accept.

Which isn't going to happen because I have a few weeks to make her fall in love with me again.

"If you couldn't be in the lab, what would you do?"

Ashton stares off as she purses her lips. "I don't know. How sad is that?"

"I don't think it's sad," I tell her with honesty. "I feel the same way. If I couldn't be a SEAL, I don't know what I'd do. Maybe I'd work for Jackson, which would be the closest I could be to actually doing what I love."

She tilts her head. "I guess I would teach. I love that part of my job. When we have a small change that leads to a breakthrough. Having something exciting that I can share gives me this immense joy. I would want to help others like that, you know?"

I have no idea what she means, but the elation on her face makes my heart pound against my chest. "I could see every guy in your class needing extra help."

"You're stupid."

"You're gorgeous."

She stops, and her smile widens. "Well, that was sweet."

"Sweet enough to earn me dinner?"

Her lips press into a thin line as she tries to hide her grin, but her eyes? They give it away. "Well, at least lunch."

"It's a start."

"Yeah, I guess it is."

chapter twenty-one

ASHTON

"AND DID YOU AGREE TO DINNER?" CLARA ASKS BEFORE SHE pops a wonton into her mouth.

"No, I didn't. Not this time. But there was a hot coffee sitting at my door when I left this morning, which was sweet."

"Yeah." She smiles. "He had to wake up early to go get it for you."

"I know, it was . . . thoughtful."

"Did you tell him?"

"Tell him about the baby?"

Clara throws a fortune cookie at me. "No, I figured you didn't do that yet. I mean did you tell him you thought it was sweet. Guys need reassurance, and Lord knows you're the worst at that."

She's not wrong, but I bristle in my seat anyway. "No, I'll do that though."

We both fall silent, and then she brings the conversation back around to what the purpose of this lunch is. The case isn't complex, but there's been multiple issues with the eggs before. This woman has undergone so much to try to conceive, and each time, there's been a loss. I don't know how Clara handles watching someone go from elation that she's pregnant to utter devastation when something goes wrong.

"I think the last issue was with the actual embryo," I tell her as I twist my fork around the Lo Mein. "It didn't look bad under the microscope the first time, but there was a change right before we did the implantation."

Clara and I inspected it, and it was within the margin of error, plus it was the second to last egg. We both felt it would've been a mistake if we didn't try.

When she actually got pregnant, we were both beyond happy. Now, I wonder if we didn't screw up.

"Hopefully, with the measures we are all taking, the last one will have a different result," Clara says with a bit of hope.

"It's the last idea we have."

"Yeah, pregnancy is such a mystery sometimes."

Sometimes it is, and sometimes it isn't.

"Speaking of . . ." Clara grins. "How are you feeling?"

"I'm fine."

She puts her chopsticks down and her features soften. "Ashton, let's be honest here. You're not fine. You called out of work yesterday to tour New York City. You're having a baby, and that's a big deal. Not to mention the guy is now courting you."

That's funny. "Courting me?"

"Well, what the hell would you call it?"

I don't know, trying to get back in my good graces, which he's actually accomplishing.

"He bought me flowers."

"Yes, he did. And he's given you coffee, talked to your parents, gave you some orgasms . . ."

"Thanks for reminding me," I say as I lean back in my

chair. "I don't know, Clara. It scares me to let him in. I wish it were all just a little simpler."

Clara smiles. "Nothing is ever simple."

"Ain't that the truth."

"I'm not trying to make you sad. I only want to make sure you know what you're giving up if you push him away. Not everyone who gets accidentally pregnant has it happen with a guy who loves her and is willing to fight for her."

She's right. He wants to fight, but he doesn't know what he's up against. Will things change? Will he run away? Will he even stay long enough to find out the news before he heads back and signs the papers? I don't know. He is a SEAL who loves his job, and I'm not sold that he means it when he says that he loves me more.

Quinn has talked about weakness, and I worry a child will be the ultimate one.

"I appreciate it, but Quinn will walk away because we don't want the same things. This is what he does when it comes to me. I'll give him credit that this has lasted longer than the last time, and he's definitely trying new methods, but I don't know. I'm focusing on the baby and the fact that I saved a boatload of cash and got what I wanted."

She releases a heavy sigh and then leans forward. "I'm happy for you. I envy that you're getting something you want. My husband never wanted kids, and at the time, I didn't either. Especially thanks to the way I grew up. I thought I would be like my mother, and . . . well . . . time has a way of changing the things you want. By the time I did want to have kids, it was too late for me. I think it worked out okay, though. I could never have been half the doctor I am if I was trying to raise a family."

"Do you regret it?"

Her dark brown eyes look away before coming back to me.

"Mac and I thought about it for a minute last year, but he's working so much at the bank, I'm here . . . it wouldn't work. I don't know that I regret it, but I think my daddy wishes I gave him grandkids. To answer your question though, no, I don't regret it. I wanted the career, and a family was on the backburner."

It's the one part that worries me too. I work insane hours. Sometimes, I'm here for fourteen hours a day when we're really busy. There are times I need to come in the middle of the night because an alarm or something goes off. I don't know how I'll do any of this and take care of a child, but I'll do it.

Quinn will be in Virginia Beach or wherever because it's not like he'll stick around, so I need to think through everything.

My chest starts to tighten and my throat is dry. The realization hits me so hard I'm shocked I don't fall off the chair. Holy shit. I'm going to be a single mom when I work like a maniac. How am I going to do this?

"Do you think I'll have to step down?" I ask her with a shake in my voice.

"Why would you?"

"I'll have a kid and . . . I don't know how I'm going to run the lab."

Clara moves to the chair beside me. "Things might change a bit, but it'll be for the better. I think we work too hard and forget to live. If it weren't for Mac, I would never leave this place. It's important to have something to live for, not work to live for. Do you know what I mean?"

I understand it completely. "It's part of what was so easy with Quinn and me for a while."

"How so?"

"He lived in Virginia Beach and was deployed all the time. It was easy to keep my life exactly as it was. I didn't have to worry about him or his time because when we did see each other, it was in short bursts. Now, he has this idea that we could build a life together, but I think that scares me too. He has this twisted version of what that looks like, you know? He has the most jacked-up family life, and I don't know that the two of us can co-parent. It's just . . . it's impossible. I wanted a baby, not a baby with Quinn after I let him go."

Or was this what I wanted somewhere in the depths of my heart all along? Last night was great and he's being sweet and wonderful, but for how long? How do I trust him or myself?

She nods. "It's definitely hard, but if you love him, it will be worth it. Plus, did you ever really let him go?"

Who the hell knows? "I thought I did."

"But he's back now and, yesterday sounds like it was what you needed."

"We had a good day, but I'm not ready to make any decisions on what that means for us. I have more than myself to think about now."

Everything was so easy for us. I smiled and laughed as we walked around New York. We had lunch at this little pizza place. It was probably the best pizza I've ever had, too. We were walking out of Central Park, saw a sign, and ate.

Then we walked back to my apartment, he kissed me on the cheek, and that was it.

"Then maybe there will be more good days."

I release a heavy sigh. "I don't trust us, Clara. I don't believe that this is magically going to be a different relationship."

"Maybe it won't, but will you forgive yourself if you don't find out?"

My heart sinks because I already know the answer. No, I never will forgive myself. A few years ago, that man stole my heart, and I've never actually gotten it back—no matter what lies I've tried to convince myself of.

"I really hope so."

"Yeah." Clara sighs. "Me too."

I flop on the couch, legs sprawled out, arms limp at my sides after one *half* of a workout, which means I walked the Brooklyn Bridge—at a leisurely pace. To be honest, I'm not exactly the workout type, but I figure if I'm about to gain a ton of weight, what I can shed now is only going to help later. Still, I'm a little tired, it's hard to walk and talk to your friends on the phone at the same time.

There's a knock at the door, and I groan. I ordered McDonald's after my trying to exercise experience, but now I have to get up to get it. Since I burned all those calories, it's only natural that this is the best time to eat junk food.

"You're ear—" I stop talking because it's not my delivery. It's Quinn.

"I'm what?"

"Irritating is the first thing that comes to mind."

He grins because, at this point, insults are like a love language between us. "How was work?"

"Fine . . . what are you doing here?"

"Visiting."

"I guess it's better than stalking."

Quinn chuckles. "Yeah. Listen, I would like it if we could have that dinner you eluded to. It's around that time, and I'm hungry."

"I can't."

"Can't or won't?"

Both. "Can't. I already ordered delivery."

Quinn shakes his head. "Okay, I'll do the same from wherever you ordered. We can have dinner here."

"Yes, we could, but I didn't invite you."

He shrugs and enters without being invited. "Semantics. What did you get? And why are you all sweaty?" Quinn asks.

The whole not liking to lie thing is pretty irritating. Quinn is the workout God. He's in the gym every freaking day. If I tell him I'm even the slightest bit into fitness, he'll have me on some crazy plan that no human being who likes sugar and bagels could survive.

Not to mention, whatever rationale I have about eating fast food isn't one he would ever support.

Mr. Eat Clean is going to lose his top. "I worked out—kind of. Oh, and I ordered McDonald's." I grab my phone to open the app. "What would you like me to add on for you, pumpkin? Since you're joining me and all."

His face is priceless. I can't tell if he's going to throw up or actually go along with it. Quinn believes his body is a temple and the only thing going inside is to further enhance his health.

I, on the other hand, could live on fries and wine. It does help that I inherited my mother's ability to eat anything she wants and not gain a pound. Even if that weren't the case, I still think I would want to enjoy food.

"I'm not really . . ."

"Oh, but you wanted to have dinner, pookie. It would be rude for you to suddenly decide otherwise, no?"

His eyes narrow. "You're right, darling, what was I thinking? I'll take a salad."

I make a clicking noise with my tongue. "Damn, they're all out."

"Of salad?"

I nod. "It's a nationwide issue with lettuce. Something about Ebola."

"I think you mean E. coli, but sure."

"Same shit. They've got chicken nuggets, burgers, fried chicken . . ." I rattle off options.

"Anything grilled?"

I turn my head and smirk. "What do you think?"

Of course they have salads and grilled chicken, but I'm not going to clue him in. "You're trying to kill me."

"Yes, yes I am. It seems that might be the only way to get rid of you."

Quinn walks over, lazy smile playing across his lips. "Here we were, getting along, had a good day yesterday, and you have to go and say mean things."

Please. I know better than that. "Have I offended your delicate senses?"

He laughs. "I'll show you how non-delicate I am."

As much as that sounds like fun, my legs are still wobbly and I stink. "Slow your roll there, Ladykiller, let's start with dinner."

He gives me the healthiest version of fast food he can manage while I smile. It's definitely not what I'm ordering him, and then we head to the living room.

"So, what did you do today?" I ask.

"You mean since I no longer have the joy of following you around?"

"Pretty much."

"Well, I woke up, attempted to go for a run but my leg was acting up. I spoke with Jackson and Mark for about two hours about some ideas I had. Then I called my commanding officer and officially put my discharge paperwork in. After that, I spoke with my doctor about the pain in my leg, cleaned the apartment a little . . ."

"Wait, wait, wait!" I say because I didn't hear much after his call with the commander. "You put your discharge paperwork in?"

I don't want to hope. I wrestle with allowing that small piece of me to gather any strength because I've been disappointed too many times. He can't get out of the navy. It would give me no more excuses as to why this will never work. He'll ruin everything.

But then . . . he'd be out.

"I did. Do you want to know why?" *Please don't say me.* "Because I don't want it anymore. I want to get a job where I don't worry about bombs and stray bullets. I want to start a life where I can have a family, a wife, and kids."

This is too much. "Quinn . . . you say this now because I'm not falling all over you, but how will you feel in a few months? What about when you have this family and you miss the action?"

"Do you think Jackson, Mark, Ben, or any of those don't see action?"

I get up and take a few steps back. Nothing is going to be any different. He'll work for Cole Security . . . in Virginia Beach or freaking California. I'll still be here in New York with a baby and broken dreams of the life he painted.

That hope I thought I could smother down didn't stay there. If it had, I wouldn't feel like I got punched in the face again.

"No, I mean, I'm sure they do . . . clearly, they do, I mean one was shot the other abducted, so yeah . . . Cole Securities is a great work environment."

He studies me and then gets to his feet. "You don't seem at all happy."

"Why would it matter how I seem?"

Quinn steps closer. "Because I'm doing this for you . . . for us."

"By getting out of the navy and living in Virginia Beach?"

"By doing what you asked me. You said you wanted me to stop deploying. You said you wanted to start living a life with a man who wasn't always leaving."

I nod and clench my teeth. "I did. But things have changed, Quinn. I've changed, and my life is changing. You need to call your commanding officer back and tell him you changed your mind . . . just like you did six months ago."

He groans and throws his hands up. "I'm trying here. I'm trying to do exactly what you want me to do so that I can show you how serious I am. I know you said we're over, what about the other day? What about the night I opened up after we had sex? I thought, oh, I don't know, that maybe there was a shot. If there wasn't, why would you even let me in a little? Why? Do you want to break my heart? Is that it? Do you want to toy with me? Is this some game?"

There are no winners here. There are just two people who can't seem to find their places. It's sad and awful. The pain of losing him was bad enough the first go around, yet here I am, enduring some form of it again.

I need to tell him. I should open my mouth and tell him that I'm pregnant. However, when I move, that's not what comes out. "No, it's not a game."

"Then why give me any fucking hope if there wasn't a chance you'd ever forgive me?"

"I wanted one last good time together!" I scream and then cover my mouth.

"What?" He takes a step closer.

My feet move backward, but there is no space because he's moving toward me. "Please, stop."

"No. Explain."

"Listen, what I said is not what you think, Quinn. I love you. I love you so much that it hurts sometimes. It's too hard to see you, touch you, or be near you and not have you. I thought that if we could have fun together, if we could maybe just become friends, then it would be so much easier for us to move on. Not that I think we'll ever be out of each other's lives—" I start to tell him. Here's my opening, but he speaks first.

"And have you . . . moved on?" His voice is a mix of fury and fear.

Answering this is almost too much because it will do nothing but make those fractures into canyons. I forgive him. It wasn't his fault completely, it was mine too, so there's nothing to forgive. But moving on? That's something else. I have to move on because he will never be the man I want him to be, and it's unfair to think he should be. While he made promises he didn't keep, I allowed myself to believe that I could change him, so I held on a bit longer.

It wasn't right of me to think that way.

And if I give him what he thinks he wants, he will only end up resenting me.

"I'm going to have a baby."

"Yes, I know this. You've told me a million times. What I'm asking is if you've moved on from me? Can you see yourself loving someone else?"

"No, not even close. But, have I moved on from the idea that we could ever be? Yeah, I guess I have."

"I see," he says as he takes a step back. "Well, then I guess I have to step up my game."

That is not exactly what I was expecting.

"Excuse me?"

"Dinner. Have dinner with me tomorrow night. A real date. You gave me lunch, now I want one dinner. One real night out, and if it goes badly, I'll walk away. I'll do whatever you want. Deal?"

One dinner, and then I tell him that I'm pregnant. He's made a deal that both of us will wish we never made. Once he finds out that he's going to be a father, he'll see that everything he's been telling himself he wants is a lie, and then he'll be gone. Just like history has shown.

chapter twenty-two

ASHTON

I STAND HERE, LOOKING AT MYSELF IN THE MIRROR, wondering how tonight will go. If it goes sideways, at least I'll look hot. My hair is down and curled at the ends so it brushes below my shoulder blades. I did my makeup a little softer since the sun bronzed my skin . . . well, maybe not bronze, but not super pale, at least, and I'm wearing my favorite blue dress.

He wouldn't tell me where we are going, just that he made reservations somewhere in case I agreed. I worry my lip, trying to calm my pounding heart. He says that this is what he wants. He freaking asked me to marry him, and now, I guess we'll see if his money's where his mouth is.

I will probably cry once I finally garner the courage to tell him he's going to be a dad.

Then I will be the one who has to make a choice.

Do I forgive him and try again?

Do I guard my heart as much as I can?

The knock at my door stops my self-reflection. "Here goes nothing," I say to the girl in the mirror. "See you on the flipside."

Once I'm through the apartment, I stand at the door, taking

two deep breaths before finding the nerve to actually turn the knob. Then, after I do, I wish I had taken two more. I've seen Quinn in many different styles of clothing. His uniform, which lasted a whole three seconds before I was ripping it off him. Jeans and T-shirt, which is my favorite because no matter how big his shirts are, they always end up looking like a smmedium—half-small, half-medium. And I've seen him at Catherine's wedding when he was in a suit.

I've never seen him in *this* suit.

Not this blue suit with a white shirt and orange tie. A suit that makes his eyes the color of sapphires that harden as they meet mine.

Not looking like he walked out of a *GQ* magazine.

This isn't fair.

This is sinful.

The way he looks right now is enough to make me want to rip both our clothes off and say fuck the food.

"You're absolutely gorgeous," he says as I stand here gaping at him.

"You're . . . you look . . . good."

No need to inflate his ego, right?

"Well, don't flatter me too much now."

I blush and glance away. He caught me in the lie and has no problems calling me on it. "Let's not pretend you're offended. You know you look very good."

He grins as though he could read my thoughts. "At least now there's a very."

Frustrating man. "Anyway, am I dressed okay? I wasn't sure what our plans were, so I sort of went casual-cute."

He steps closer, pushing my hair off my shoulder. "You're perfect. You could wear a burlap sack and be breathtaking. Or nothing at all. I always approve of naked."

I roll my eyes. He says that now, but when I'm the size of a whale, we'll see.

I try to put my pregnancy out of my mind. I need to get through tonight and then tell him. No need to destroy our first date by blurting out that I have a bun in the oven.

"I have something for you."

This grabs my attention, and I turn to him. "You do?"

Quinn reaches into his pocket and pulls out a blue box with a white ribbon wrapped around it.

I gasp and look up. His eyes are trained on mine as he extends the gift toward me.

My hand shakes, and I can't quite get myself to reach toward him. It's not a bomb, I know this, but it's *Tiffany's*.

"I saw it when we were there, and I thought it was about time that you got something," he says with a laugh. "Your entire home should've been filled with them by now."

Who knew that this box would be so hard to take?

"Quinn," I say as I look at him.

This is too much.

There's too many things going on in my head, and I'm confused and excited. He got me a blue box. Even if there's nothing inside it . . . I don't care.

Okay, that's a lie.

I totally do.

But still . . .

Slowly, my hand extends, taking it but not moving to lift the lid. I stare at it, not wanting to ruin the beauty and simplicity that it holds. A satin white ribbon is tied perfectly. I'll never be able to recreate it. If it weren't so tacky, I'd grab my phone to document this.

"Open it," he urges.

"I can't."

"You can't open it?"

I shake my head. "No, because no matter what it is, this box will never be the same."

Quinn looks at me as though I'm nuts, which I am, but he doesn't get it. This is a box women would buy just to have. It's dumb and materialistic, but there's something about this brand that makes chicks a little stupid.

"Then I'll open it."

I snatch my hand back and slap his with my other. "Don't touch it."

His smile is wide. "Then please, *fragolina*, before we miss our reservation, see what I got you."

There's an impatience in his voice I haven't heard before. Is he nervous? That's freaking cute. "Fine." I gently pull on the ribbon and then lift the lid. Inside is a little Tiffany-Blue bag. I smile as I open it and see a silver ring. It's an infinity symbol.

"When I saw it," Quinn starts talking, "I couldn't help thinking about what an infinity sign means. There's no beginning and there is no end." He takes the ring from my fingers and puts it on me. "Sort of like us. We didn't have a beginning, and I never want there to be an end."

Oh, my freaking heart is melting.

My fingers shake as I look at it until the tears are so thick the ring becomes too hard to see. I lift my gaze back to his, and then his palms are cupping my cheeks and his thumbs are softly wiping away the tears. My heart is pounding so hard I can't breathe.

I can't go on this date without telling him.

There is no way I can endure any kind of public . . . anything.

Plus, he says he doesn't want an end, but what if this is the end? What if, when I tell him that he's going to have a kid, he sees that his entire life will alter and decides he doesn't want it?

Quinn grew up with an asshole father and a mother who

wasn't worth the air she breathed. He's said time and time again that having a child when you're not ready isn't fair to the kid. Sure, I was ready and I would never be the kind of mother that he had, but I don't think he is ready.

I have to say it.

"Ashton?" he calls my name while tears continue to fall.

I wanted a date, but it's not fair to do to him.

"Why are you crying, sweetheart?" Quinn asks with a soft laugh.

Because I'm about to ruin everything.

My lips part, chest heaving as another tear slides down my face. "I'm pregnant."

His head jerks back as though he's been struck. "Already? You went through with a procedure? Already?"

Oh, how I wish it were that way. Then he wouldn't look at me like I kicked him. "No." My voice is soft and sounds deflated. "Not already. Not like that."

"But you . . . I was gone a few fucking days!"

"Quinn, listen to me," I say with more strength than I feel. "I'm saying that *we're* pregnant. You and me. Us. It's your baby."

He looks at me, but it's more like he's looking through me. As though the words I'm saying aren't really registering in his mind, which I understand because I pretty much had my own out-of-body experience when I found out.

Being told you're having a baby when you weren't actually trying isn't easy to digest.

Quinn's eyes gloss over, and he doesn't say a word.

I move my hand in front of his face, but he doesn't so much as blink.

I think I broke him. Who knew? The guy who keeps calm in war has a weakness: unplanned pregnancy.

"I'll wait," I say and then sigh.

166 | CORINNE MICHAELS

"I'm just . . ."

"Yeah."

He shakes his head. "You're sure?"

"Yup. I'm sure. We're having a baby."

His eyes open and close a few times as though he's escaping whatever fog he was in. "Okay. A baby. I wasn't expecting that."

"Oh, neither was I when I went to the clinic for the medication to get pregnant."

Quinn moves over toward the couch and then leans against it. "How are you feeling?"

"Conflicted."

The word hangs around us, but at least it's honest. I'm happy because I wanted a baby, and in a part of my heart, it has always been him I've wanted one with. He's the man I would've built a life around, and here we are, kind of doing it.

Just not the way we thought.

"What about physically? Are you okay? Is the baby okay?"

I move closer to him and nod softly. "We're all okay as far as I can tell. I'm very early on. So much so that a home pregnancy test probably wouldn't have picked it up. If one did, it would've been difficult to read and I would have still had to go to the clinic for confirmation."

He stands straight as though to move closer to me but then stops. "We didn't use a condom."

"No, and I've been off the pill for a bit."

Slowly, a smile creeps across his face.

"Why are you smiling? I'm a mess!"

"I'm not," he says after a second.

"You're not what?"

"Conflicted or a mess. I'm . . . I don't know . . . relieved?"

Now, I've heard it all.

"You're relieved that we're going to have a baby?"

When Quinn moves again, he doesn't hesitate as he takes my hand in his. "Yeah. I love you, Ashton Caputo. I love you, and I hated the idea of you ever having another man's baby. Would I have done what you needed if it happened that way? Yes. Would I have fucking hated it? Yup. Do I love the fact that you're going to have a baby with me? Yes, yes I do. The fact that *I* got you pregnant . . . I'm fucking elated. I mean it when I say I don't want us to have an end."

I glance at the ring that sits on my finger, the one symbolizing a never-ending loop. In some ways, it is our relationship. We go around and around and never find the finish line.

"I'm a little stunned," I say with honesty. "I wasn't sure how you'd take it, but relief or joy definitely weren't high on my list of possibilities."

He brings his hand to my cheek. "Ashton, I'm a fuck up. We know this. I've given you every reason to distrust me, but I vow, right here, that I will be a better man. And if that man isn't someone you can love, then know that I'll be a good father to our baby."

That is the one thing I never doubted. "How about you just be you? We have about eight months to get our shit together one way or another," I offer.

"Are you happy at all, *fragolina*?" Quinn pushes a stray piece of hair from my face, tucking it behind my ear.

His touch is so soft and reverent that my defenses drop. That simple movement is a tenderness I've yearned for.

"I've been afraid to be," I admit to him. He's been open, honest, and maybe he has changed but I've been too defiant to believe it. "It's what I wanted, I mean . . . I was willing to do artificial insemination to get a baby. But, to know it's us and you, there's a relief there too. I was scared of what would happen if you had reacted badly to the news, though. I didn't want to be upset, so I sort of tempered my emotions around it."

Now, though, I let myself feel a bit more, and it's overwhelming. My body is tingly and warm as I allow the fear to be replaced with optimism. He knows, and he's taking it better than I ever could have hoped.

He watches me, his eyes studying subtle movements, and a slow smile creeps across his lips. "And now?"

Another tear forms. "Yeah, I'm happy."

"Good, let's go on our date, okay?"

"Where are we going?"

"McDonald's."

I burst out laughing, tears no longer filling my eyes. I'm pretty sure I just fell head over heels in love with him again.

chapter twenty-three

I WASN'T REALLY TAKING HER TO McDONALD'S. I ONLY ATE IT before because she pretty much dared me, knowing I don't back down. She was so sure I would find my way out of it, and I loved watching her smug smile disappear.

Now, though, I'm wondering if I shouldn't cancel the Italian restaurant in the Theater District and take her for some fries. I will if it's going to make her smile at me like that again.

We head out of the building, and she slides her arm into the crook of mine. I do everything I can to not make it seem like a big deal, but it is because she's touching me without me having to push her.

"You know, the whole fast food thing was a joke, right?"

She smiles. "I figured, but I was a little excited."

"Tonight is about you and us, and I want to spoil you a little, is that okay?"

"Yeah, that's okay."

The hope is that tonight will go so well that I can take her on a million more dates. I can finally prove that I have changed and stop telling her. Apparently, actions do speak louder than words, and I've been a little too slow on the uptake to actually do that when it comes to Ashton.

And then I remember . . . we're having a baby.

Ashton and I are having a child. Not some random guy in a book, but *us*.

When I was determined not to allow that to happen, I didn't think this would be the path we would take, but I'm happy it is.

"Quinn?" she says after we get down the subway stairs.

Jesus, I don't even remember getting here. It's as though I'm in a fog. One that's filled with possibilities.

"Yeah?"

"Are you seriously okay?"

I laugh once. "I am. It's not exactly what I planned as the start of our date, but it's all good."

She smiles. "No, I imagine not. What did you plan?"

Most of the plan will still happen, so I don't want to give too much away. She's surprised me, so now it's my turn. "You'll see."

"Hmm." Ashton's eyes narrow. "So, you won't tell me?"

"Nope."

I have zero ideas if this is what she wants to do, and our friends were no help on this, but I dug deep to find romance, which isn't hard in a city like this.

So, here goes my best plan.

We exit the subway and start to walk. "Are your feet okay?" I ask. She's in heels, and I didn't even think of getting a car service instead of walking.

She looks at me with wonder. "Umm, yes, why?"

"I can't imagine those are comfortable."

"No, but I wear heels a lot, so I'm used to them."

"I don't know how much walking you would want to do . . ."

"I'll let you know if it gets to be too much. I mean, it's not like we're going to stroll through Central Park, right?"

I shake my head. "No, I thought about it, but I opted for something a little more glamorous."

Her smile grows bigger, and I take her hand in mine, lacing our fingers. My thumb brushes against the ring I gave her. I wasn't sure what to get when I walked in, but when I saw it, I knew. I plan to get her other things in the future.

Hell, I plan to give her so many of those blue boxes she can't count them. However, I may want to pace myself since I'm about to be unemployed. I will officially be out of the navy in one month thanks to the meeting with Commander Thomas and Master Chief Schaffer. Between my medical leave and accumulated standard leave I've had banked, I was able to get an early discharge.

Jackson and Mark have already guaranteed me a spot at Cole Securities. I'll be handling a few protective and asset details, plus, I'll be working as long-range cover for the bigger jobs.

Ashton and I walk a few more blocks and make it to the restaurant a few minutes late. They seat us immediately, and I sort of dig the vibe here.

It's that old-school Italian where there is a rose and candles on the tables, and each table has a chandelier with a drapery on it to soften the ambiance . . . at least I think that's why.

"You know, I've always wanted to eat here," she says as she looks around.

"Really?"

She nods quickly. "This is the place where everyone goes to before a show. It's sort of a ritual."

I read that on the reservation site. All the reviews were raving about the food and proximity to Broadway, which is exactly where we're going after.

"Well, at least I can check another first off your list."

She leans back. "What else did you check off?"

I go to say that I got her knocked up first, but then I re-member that's not true. That stupid dickhead who should be castrated did. Hopefully, the big firsts will be mine. I've already ticked one off in the form of a blue box. The others, like her having a child, getting married, living with a man, I want just as much. "You know one, you're wearing it now."

"True. What else?"

I sit there, a little stunned. "You know, I'm not sure. Had any other man taken you to Central Park?"

She bites her lower lip while lifting her shoulders. "Just once."

"Okay, well, I've got Tiffany's and now here."

Ashton laughs and takes a sip of her water. "I'm happy we've at least got this one—and the other."

"Me too."

It's now my goal to check every last one off. I'm going to win her, come hell or high water.

chapter twenty-four

ASHTON

DINNER IS GREAT, WE KEEP IT LIGHT BECAUSE I HONESTLY can't think about anything heavy. I feel like that's all we are—heavy. Everything with us has been overly intense, and I wonder how much blame falls on me.

I wanted it all, and I wanted it now.

I'm about to get all that I wanted and more than I could've ever hoped for.

However, tonight has been great. He took the news of the pregnancy in stride, which is more than I ever hoped for. He's been sweet and kind . . . and the ring.

Infinity.

The things he said when he gave it to me were almost too much.

"Hey." Quinn grabs my hand, covering the silver mathematical sign.

"Sorry."

"Do you want to call it a night?" he asks. "I'm sure you're . . ."

"No," I tell him quickly. I don't want this night to end because I'm a basket case. Dinner made it possible for me to avoid thinking too much. We talked about Virginia Beach, our friends—especially Liam and Natalie. I have to remember to send them a gift for the advice they gave him. He told me a little about going to visit his buddies who are in rehab.

When I look at Quinn, it's sometimes easy to forget that he's not as strong as he likes to pretend he is. He may be this big guy that everything tends to bounce off him, but I know the inside. The walls don't come down often, but I've been there when they have.

It's hard to carry the world on your shoulders and expect them never to get tired.

Quinn gives me a smile. "Good. Are you ready for the next part of our date?"

"I am."

He stands and then extends his hand to help me up. "Who knew you were a gentleman?"

"I have many hidden talents."

"I'm pretty sure I know the ones that matter."

"I'm sure you do," he says under his breath.

We head back out into the muggy New York summer night, and he takes my hand in his. It's funny how such a small gesture can do so many things. It can be a sign of support and solidarity or comfort when you need it, but in this moment, it's more. Quinn's hand in mine is a sign of all of those things and a promise. He's here. He's holding my hand, showing me that he's beside me.

Maybe for him it doesn't mean that, but it feels like it does. And I like it.

A lot more than I should.

"Where are we going?" I ask as we make a right onto 7th Ave.

"You'll see."

As we walk, I recall what I said about Times Square at night.

I smile because even though I live here and I grew up in Jersey where coming to the city wasn't such a big deal, I still love it.

It's a place you can see a million times, and it will never be the same experience. Sure enough, the lights get brighter the closer we walk.

"I know you think this is where we're going," Quinn says as we get to the center. "But it's not."

"No?" I ask with a bit of curiosity.

I would've sworn this was his big plan.

"Nope."

Okay, now he really does have me intrigued.

We keep going, but both of our eyes dart around the space as the thirty-second ads move onto the next. Catherine once told me what her client spent on one of those ads, and I almost passed out. The cost to be seen by that many people is astronomical. Since then, I've done my best to pay attention because if they ever figure out it doesn't work, then what would I look at?

We keep walking and then make a right onto 51st Street. Broadway? No way is Quinn Miller going to take me to a show. There must be some other thing he has planned.

"Are your feet okay?" he asks as I stumble a bit.

"I'm fine," I say with a smile. I love that he's being so concerned, but I've walked miles in heels and have lived to tell about it. Sure, I'm a little uncomfortable, but it's nothing I can't handle. His legs are so damn long that I have to take two steps to each of his one to keep up.

"Here," he says and then swoops low, lifting me into his arms. My arms wrap around his neck, more from surprise and instinct than anything.

"What are you doing?" I ask with a gasp.

"Taking care of you."

"Put me down." Trying to wiggle out of his arms is useless.

He holds me with the ease and security he would use to hold a bouquet of flowers.

"You're walking slow, which means your feet hurt. And you're having my baby, so just hold on to me. I won't let you fall."

So many things ping around in my head.

I've already fallen.

Please don't ever put me down.

God, it feels good to be in your arms.

But, mostly, I wonder how I'll get through tonight without being right back where we started. Me in love with him, hoping for a life he says he'll give me but can't.

I know he's saying all the right things, and I'd be lying to myself if I said I didn't wish they were all true. Because, God, do I ever. I struggle to believe him because he's said similar things in the past.

He hasn't ever turned in his discharge papers before, though.

Or told me he loves me.

Or bought me jewelry.

Quinn walks with the same pace he was without having an extra buck thirty in his arms. We get in front of the Gershwin Theater, and he stops. "Here we are."

"You're kidding me," I say with a wide grin. "You're taking me to a show?"

"I am."

"And which of my lovely friends do I have to thank for this?" I ask.

He shakes his head, nose brushing my hair. "None, *frago-lina*. No one helped me with tonight. This is me, proving to you that I know you."

My eyes meet his. "And how is that?"

Quinn doesn't move his gaze as the words fall from his lips.

"Italian food is your favorite, which is why we went there. Your favorite movie is *The Wizard of Oz,* and you can basically recite the entire movie."

I don't know how he remembers that.

As if seeming to read my thoughts, he speaks again. "Do you not remember the first night we spent together? I do. I remember everything about it."

Suddenly, his arms feel too tight. I forgot about it. I was so broken, sad, and ashamed at myself. "Quinn . . ."

"We sat in my room and watched it with you in my arms. You cried off and on and talked about how great it would be to close your eyes and follow the yellow brick road. I remember not understanding a damn thing because I was trying so hard not to want to kiss you. You said that having something laid out in front of you would make things easier."

"I lied. Nothing worth having is that easy," I tell him.

It's true. No path is ever easy. Nothing in life is freaking easy. I thought I could find that stupid brick road by having my own baby without a man. I would give up the idea of a family that clearly didn't exist. My life would be the path I paved.

But Quinn came back, I got pregnant, and now I'm in his arms on a busy street because he didn't want my feet to hurt.

"No, nothing is, but when you found me, I was the Tin Man. I was hollow on the inside."

He says it as though it's no longer true. "And now?"

"Now, I found out I had a heart. You've had it this whole time."

The heart that beats in my chest races. I release my hold from around his neck, and Quinn takes the hint. He sets me back on the ground, his eyes are unreadable, and I know he must take that as a rejection.

Slowly, my hands run up his chest and return back to their

place around his neck. I lean forward, kissing him slowly as the world moves around us. It's a short kiss, but I hope it conveys how much all of this means to me.

When I move back, breaking our connection, I give him a soft smile. "I see you also found your courage."

Quinn chuckles. "I'd say my brain has also been located."

Not wanting to give him too much confidence, I shrug. "I guess we'll find out."

The show is amazing. Beyond amazing. I cried, of course. I'm a girl and my heart was never lost. I'm pretty sure he did as well, but then again, he's a master at disguising emotion when he needs to.

I'm on cloud nine . . . or maybe ten, if that's a thing.

"I still can't breathe," I say as we exit the theater. "The love and the heartbreak. I just . . ."

"It was a great show," he admits almost begrudgingly.

"Yeah, it was. My little Oz-loving heart is overjoyed."

"I'm glad."

This has been the best date of my life. "Thank you," I say as we move back into the throngs of people.

"For?"

"Everything. The dinner, the date, the walk, the show, and not to mention how you took my big bomb drop."

He pulls me to his side, one arm wrapped around my shoulders as I press closer to him. We walk like a couple in love, which maybe we are. I don't know. Whatever we are, I don't want to focus on it this second.

I want to enjoy the moment.

Us.

"Did I impress you?" Quinn asks as we find seats on the subway, still wrapped up around each other.

"Very much. Who knew under all that stupid was a guy that was so romantic?"

He smiles and laughs but I can still see the questions swirling in his gaze. When his attention drops to my lips, I know he wants to kiss me. I want it, too, but now that we're flying away from the hustle of the city and back to my reality in Brooklyn, I wonder if I should.

While tonight was a night I'll not soon forget, it doesn't mean that our lives are less complicated.

My head and heart are struggling for the choice, and because no one side wins out, I turn and look away.

It's not because I don't love him. It's because I love him so much that I wouldn't survive another loss.

He's the one guy I can't seem to quit.

"Ashton." Quinn barely whispers my name.

"Yes?" The fear in my voice doesn't go unmissed.

"I don't want you to be afraid anymore. I know I have to earn your trust again. When we get back to your place, I have one last surprise."

My eyes narrow because that's not a surprise. I'm well acquainted with what he wants to do in my apartment. I even have the baby as a souvenir.

"I bet you do."

He laughs, despite the seriousness of a few seconds ago. "Not *that*—although, I won't turn you away. Looking at you all night has been . . . hard."

The dirty jokes float through my brain. "I'm not going to apologize if I'm making things hard on you."

I look at his crotch. I really do love his dick. Maybe one more night won't be a mistake. It's not like I can get pregnant—again.

Enjoying sex after a night like this would be a reasonable thing to do, right?

"Oh, I'll show you hard," he grumbles with his lips to my ear. "I'll show you how very, very hard things can get."

I try to smother my shiver, but I fail. Whatever. It's not like he doesn't know how much I enjoy sex with him.

"We should probably stop," I suggest.

Quinn shifts in his seat, but he doesn't let me go. "I promise to be a gentleman. I just would like this next part to be in private."

I have no idea what it could be, but it seems to matter to him. I worry my bottom lip and then nod. "Okay."

Then I say a silent prayer to the heavens that this isn't another let down.

"Why don't you go change, you can't be comfortable," Quinn suggests as he shrugs out of his suit jacket.

"Now you're scaring me."

Why would it matter what I'm wearing?

He runs his hand down his face and releases a groan. "I'm . . . it's nothing bad, Ashton. Just, I hate seeing you uncomfortable all night."

Was I uncomfortable? I don't think so. Sure, the dress kept riding up and my boobs are so freaking sore that I couldn't wear a bra, but I didn't think that was anything big.

"Do I need to change for this talk? I'd rather not delay it since my overactive imagination has conjured a million different possibilities."

He rolls his eyes, probably seeing that my patience is non-existent and he's going to lose this fight. "No, I guess not."

"Okay then, talk."

Quinn doesn't do that though, he takes a paper out of his pants pocket, and unfolds it. Then, he takes two strides over to me and extends it. "Here, I wanted to show you this."

What the hell is it? Maybe it's a warrant for his arrest. Or a deed to a house. Oh, or it could be a letter saying he won some kind of prize. Maybe it's a paternity test for another girl he wooed. With Quinn, I never know.

However, of all the other possibilities I thought of. None of them prepared me for this.

I look up, my eyes meeting his and my lips parted. "This is a discharge paper."

"Yes."

"From the navy."

"Yes."

"With your name on it," I say, needing to keep clarifying each point.

"It is. I'm officially out in thirty days. I'm technically on leave, and I don't have to go back, so I guess, I'm out now," he rambles.

My gaze drops to the paper again, waiting for the joke to finally hit. "You . . . got out of the navy?"

"I told you before that I talked to my commander."

I nod. He did, but talking to and getting discharge papers from are two different things. This isn't some abstract thought or hope. This is concrete. This is signed, sealed, delivered and he doesn't ever have to go back.

My heart is pounding. "I . . . I can't believe it."

He steps closer, his hand touches my chin, lifting it gently to look at him. "I know that part of what our issues were before was that I didn't talk to you about whether I should've stayed in or out. You wanted to be an active participant in our life together, and I wasn't listening to you. I realize that I did that again, but I did it because I wanted you to know that I was doing it without any assurances that you were going to be with me. I wanted you to know that I love you enough to take that risk. I've broken promises. I've failed you, and I need to prove to you that I won't make those mistakes again."

My heart races. He did all of this before he even knew there was a baby. He chose me, which is all I ever wanted. He told me he'd done it, but I didn't believe he would go through with it.

A tear falls down my cheek, and he wipes it away.

"Why are you crying?" Quinn's voice is soft.

"Because . . ." I try to find the words to describe it. I don't know why. There are so many different reasons.

"Because?"

I can see how uncertain he is, and that only makes me feel more things. Quinn is always the steady legs in the rough seas. He's the guy who knows what he wants and makes the choice, damn the consequences.

Now, he doesn't seem so sure of anything.

"Because," I make another attempt. "Because you confuse me! I love you and then I don't and then I love you and I don't want to. I want to have a baby and then you knock me up! Here I was, worried about everything with you in the military and us having a baby, but then you take me on this date. Not just dinner and a show, but a show that you chose because of me. Because you remembered something about me and my heart. Why can't you go back to being an idiot who didn't love me?" I shout the last part and try to move away.

Quinn doesn't let me. He grips my arms, holding me right there. "I was never an idiot who didn't love you. I was an idiot who didn't tell you."

And right there is the exact moment that Quinn broke the very last part of my walls.

chapter twenty-five

ASHTON

"KISS ME," I SAY BREATHLESSLY.

He doesn't ask again or give me any chance to change my mind. His lips press against mine, and I soften against him. My hands travel up his thick arms, his neck, and then to the back of his head. I hold him, drinking in the glorious way he attacks my mouth.

Our lips move together, and it's as if I've finally come home.

I was a fool to think I'd end up anywhere but here.

He's the person who I've wanted, and he's giving me everything I want. I can't possibly turn it down.

We're lost in each other for a few moments, and I want to give him something this time. I don't want another screw on the couch, not that it wasn't fabulous, but this time, I want it to be more than that.

Giving myself to him, freely and without restraint.

"Quinn," I say against his lips.

"What, sweetheart?"

I preen at the term of endearment. "Come with me," I say as I drop my hand to his.

We walk wordlessly to my bedroom.

As much as I'd like to say that I didn't anticipate this, that would be bullshit. I cleaned, made sure there were fresh flowers on the dresser, and strategically placed candles in the room—a girl has to plan for any possibility.

And, yet, none of that is noticed. Quinn is focused solely on me. "You're so damn gorgeous."

"You make me feel pretty."

"Why is that?" he asks as he circles around me, finger grazing against the skin of my collarbone.

"The way you look at me," I admit. "The way you kiss me."

He stops behind me, his arm hooking around my front and his lips gliding along my neck. "There's no other woman in the world who can hold a candle to you, Ashton. You're the sun, the flames, the stars, the heat that consumes this world."

My head falls back to his shoulder, and I close my eyes. It's nice to feel adored. "And aren't you afraid to get burned?"

Quinn rubs his nose along my ear, the warmth of his breath causing my flesh to break out in goose bumps. "I welcome the burn, *fragolina*. Your fire doesn't destroy, it gives me life." Then his hand moves down to my belly, resting there. "Look at what your warmth gave us."

I still struggle with how genuinely happy he seems about this. "How are you this okay with it?"

He turns me so I can see his face. "When you told me you wanted to have another man's child, I thought I would lose my mind. It was then that I knew I would do anything to be the man who gave it to you. I'm okay with it because I want this with you. I want everything with you."

My fingers lift, touching his face. "For how long?"

He shakes his head as though I'm missing the obvious. "Indefinitely."

Our lips crash together in haste. There are no more words

because anything he says after that, I don't want to hear. His hands are on my neck, controlling my head, moving me from side to side. It's a sign of power and control, one I welcome.

His tongue slides into my mouth, pushing and fighting for dominance. Quinn's fingers glide against my neck and cup my breasts, squeezing, and I push back in pain. Well, pregnancy joy number one.

Quinn takes a few steps back, confusion sweeping across his gorgeous face.

"Really fucking tender," I explain.

His eyes are filled with understanding as he moves back to me. "Then I'll have to pay attention to other things."

Heat fills my body, warming every inch of skin, every ounce of blood. "Yeah?"

He takes another step as I move back, legs hitting the bed. "Want me to show you?"

"Very much so."

"Take your dress off while I watch."

My hand reaches behind me, slowly sliding the zipper lower. I might like when he's bossy in bed, but I like teasing him. When he gets broody, it's fucking hot, and nothing makes him react more than when I toy with him.

The sound of the metal teeth coming apart sets him on edge. He clenches his hands at his sides, and I don't do anything but take my time.

His chest rises and falls a little harder as we stare at each other. He knows exactly what I'm doing, and I wait for him to snap.

One.

Two.

Three.

Quinn moves with lightning speed, his hands push mine aside as he releases the zipper and pulls the dress from my body.

He leans down, fingers gripping the back of my thighs as I grab his arms for support. Normally, he'd toss my ass onto the bed, but he slows himself.

"I don't want to fuck you tonight." His voice is low and gruff, restraint in every syllable.

"Then what exactly do you want?" Because I would very much like that.

He lays me on the bed softly, as though I'm a delicate flower he's afraid to break.

Quinn's eyes are intense as he climbs over me. "I want to worship you."

Well, that sounds just fine to me.

Then I realize what he means by that. He wants to make love. He wants us to join together, not in anger or in one of our typical very hot and sweaty sex sessions but in a slow show of emotions. Quinn wants to show me more.

I don't welcome the tears that pool because I'm clearly an emotional idiot, but they come anyway. "Make love to me, Quinn," I say the words, and then he kisses me.

His lips are no less intense, but there's something else between us. An understanding that this is different. Everything about tonight has been the same way. It wasn't our normal time together. It was filled with smiles and . . . love.

We kiss, but then his mouth starts to move. He kisses my neck, shoulders, and down my chest.

While my breasts are sore, they're also very sensitive in a way they've never been before. When his tongue slides over my nipple, I could come right there.

He reads my body, always aware of things that I don't think he could know, and does it again, this time making a circle.

"Jesus." I breathe the word.

Quinn does the same to the other, causing another moan to escape my mouth.

He keeps doing it until my hips are moving, needing more, needing him.

I ache with desire. My limbs are tight, and my fingers dig into his back. "I'm so close."

He chuckles against my skin. "We may break a record tonight."

I don't think I'll mind this one bit. If pregnant sex is like this, I may get knocked up again just to keep it.

"Please, baby," I whimper, internally groaning at the sound of my own voice.

"Be patient, *fragolina*," Quinn's lust-filled tone urges as he moves lower.

Oh, I'm so not going to be patient if that's what he's doing. Nothing in this world comes close to the feel of his mouth on me.

He slowly moves down my body, lingering over my belly as his lips press there gently. He descends farther and then his tongue makes a torturously slow swipe against my core. My back arches, eyes closed, as he does it again. "You taste like heaven."

"You feel like heaven," I tell him.

"Well, let's see if we can make the angels sing."

And sing they do. I cry out his name as he makes circles around my clit. My hands fist the comforter as he pumps a finger into my pussy while his mouth sucks and flicks the nerves that drive me wild.

I don't even fight it.

I come so hard that I'm not sure I'm even tethered to this earth anymore. A sheen of sweat covers my chest, and I'm panting.

He's back to eye level and he's trying to hide the smirk on his lips. The man should be proud. That was freaking fantastic.

"And now what are you going to do?" I ask him.

His answer is to slide into me, filling me to the hilt. I grip his shoulders, trying to accommodate for the intrusion.

"Are you okay?" he asks through gritted teeth.

"Yes."

"The baby?"

I look at him, brows furrowed. "Huh?"

"I just . . . I mean, I'm not sure. If the . . . the baby."

And then I realize what he's asking. He's worried that sex will hurt the baby. "No, the baby is fine, but I won't be if you don't start moving soon."

He pushes my hair back, eyes staying on mine as he moves slow and with purpose. He fills me. Every single part of me. My heart, my lungs, my body, and my soul are all one with him.

With each thrust, I climb higher, and I never want this to stop. This is the Quinn I've been longing for. The one who cares for me, makes me feel special and valued. He gave up his career and has shown me . . .

An epiphany happens as I stare in his deep blue eyes.

For the first time, I see all the things he's done in a different light.

Maybe it wasn't the smartest strategy, but there it is. He loves me.

He loves me and the baby we made.

He loves me and wants to make me happy.

He loves me enough to do all the dumb things he could to find a way back into my heart.

And the stupid bastard accomplished it.

My fingers wrap around the back of his neck, and I pull his lips to mine. I kiss him with everything I am. I want him to feel the joy that is overtaking me. Tears leak from my lids as his lips break from mine and he stares at me. "Am I hurting you?"

"No," I say with my head shaking.

"Then why are you crying?"

"Because I love you."

His eyes light up like a kid on Christmas morning who got a pony. "I love you."

"I know."

"You do?"

I nod as my hand caresses his cheek. "Yeah, I really do."

chapter twenty-six

ASHTON

"ARE YOU SCARED?" I ASK QUINN WHILE SQUIRMING IN THE passenger seat.

"Nope."

He should be. We're in the car to see my parents for Sunday dinner—together—as a couple. Much to his dismay, I went alone last week, but I felt it was the best choice. We had only been back together for twenty-four hours and I wanted to make sure he didn't change his mind again.

"Well, I'm beyond excited about this."

He taps his thumbs on the wheel. "Why is that?"

"My father is going to castrate you for knocking his baby girl up. I don't care that he likes you, he will not like knowing that you defiled me."

This is going to be so much freaking fun.

When I called my mother to tell her I was bringing a date, she squealed and said something about prayers being answered. They have no idea it's Quinn. First, because it's been a week. Second, because they'd ask a million questions that I wasn't sure I had the answers for. Like, how long is he staying in New York? Did he find another job? Are you moving to Virginia Beach? Why aren't you married yet?

"Then we'll have to say it was a one-time thing. You know, leave out the fact that I defiled you in the shower before we left to come to dinner."

The shower. What a way to get clean.

We've had a lot of sex. Pregnancy sex didn't sound all that much fun, but the extra blood vessels do a body very good. So far, I've had none of the morning sickness or any issues other than my boobs really freaking hate my bra.

"You want to lie to the man?"

"I don't think he wants or needs details," Quinn replies.

"True." I sigh as I look out the window. "But it would make this dinner that much more enjoyable. I say we play it by ear."

Quinn ignores me and keeps driving, but not before taking my hand in his.

This has taken a bit of getting used to. He's never been overly affectionate. It wasn't as though he didn't hold my hand before, but it's almost like he can't stop himself now. He's always finding ways to touch me, ask if I'm okay, or do something for me.

It's really sweet.

Every day this week, he has walked me to work, we stopped and got breakfast, and then he'd kiss me before going back home.

Tonight, though, we are going to tell my parents the big news.

And watch my mother lose her shit.

And watch my father try to kill Quinn.

He pulls the car into the driveway and then kisses the top of my hand. "You ready?"

"Oh, I sure am. I'm pregnant, they won't beat me."

He snorts and then we exit the car.

"Mom!" I call out when I open the door. "We're here."

I hear her fuss at my father and then she comes to the door. Her eyes widen when she sees who is standing behind me. "Quinn!"

"Hi, Mrs. C." The jackass already has her grinning as he steps forward with a bouquet of flowers. He's hoping to gain her as an ally when the shit hits the fan.

"You didn't have to bring me these." My mother's cheeks turn red. "You're a sweet boy. Isn't he a sweet boy, Ashton?"

"Yes, Mom."

"And you two are back together and you didn't tell me!"

Great, she turns on me. "Me? He didn't tell you either."

She scoffs. "I'm not his mother."

"No, but apparently, he's the son you never had."

I'm over most of what happened when Quinn was working his way back into my life, but the traitors that reside in this house have some explaining to do.

My mother cocks her head to the side. "Don't be petulant, Ashton Beth. If your father and I didn't like Quinn, then how would this be? We saw how he felt about you and listened to him, which is a skill that you struggle with." She pauses and watches for a retort. "It clearly comes from your father's side, but a mother knows, my darling."

I guess I'll find out how much truth there is in that statement. "Yes, well, I don't forgive you yet."

She smiles. "I made penne ala vodka."

My mother is a shrewd woman. "With ravioli?"

"And garlic bread."

"With the cheese on top?" I ask.

I can't resist garlic cheese bread.

"And I made extra sauce that you can dip it in."

My stomach growls, and she grins. "Maybe I'll feel less hostile after I eat."

Mom laughs and pulls me into her arms. "I'm so happy for you."

"Me too."

Dinner is great. We all laugh and talk about what's new since they last saw Quinn. I can see this being my life—Quinn and I coming to my parents' on Sundays, the baby knowing the love of his or her grandparents, and us being happy.

It's the one thing that the two of us haven't talked about yet, though. How do we make this work?

I can't give my job up—or, at least, I don't want to.

Leaving my parents seems like the second big hurdle.

Dad clears his throat. "Son, now that you're out, what are you doing for work?"

"I'm actually going to take a job with Cole Securities."

And here we go.

"Where Gretchen works?" Dad asks, his eyes moving to mine.

"Yes, Dad, the very same."

"I see."

As do I.

"It'll be very flexible to start. Mark and Jackson will have me come when I'm needed, and I can stay here when I'm not on a detail."

My chest loosens and relief starts to form. Does this mean he'll stay in New York and only travel for work? Is that even what I want? How much will he be gone?

Quinn looks at me, his deep blue eyes feel as if they're piercing through me. I sometimes wonder if he can read my thoughts. "I'll go back and forth, but it'll give Ashton and I some time to work things out and come up with a plan."

He's . . . consulting with me?

What in the fresh hell is going on?

"You didn't mention this," I speak up, my voice trembling a bit.

"You didn't ask."

"I didn't know I should."

His jaw clenches and then relaxes. "You can ask me anything."

"Good to know."

"And then we'll discuss it," Quinn adds.

"Okay."

"And the two of us will come to an agreement—together."

My smile is slow and builds because it's everything I wanted. He's taking the two of us and making us a team.

I turn to my parents. "Mom, Dad?" My voice shakes as I address them. "Quinn and I wanted to talk to you about something."

"Oh my God!" my mother screams. "You're getting married!"

My eyes widen as I shake my head quickly. "No, no, no, we're not."

"But . . . you two have been together for so long."

"We've also been apart, and we're not getting married."

"Well, not right now," Quinn tacks on.

"You're not helping."

My mother wants a wedding more than I do. She loved helping my cousins, shopping for the dress, and the whole mother of the bride part. I'm pretty sure they have enough money saved for any extravagance I could dream of. I would've rather used that for college or anything else, but a wedding—that's Mom's dream.

"But it's the perfect time, Ashton. The summer dresses will be on display soon, and you know how I feel about summer weddings."

This is going to go off the rails very quickly. "Mom."

"And the flowers, oh, with your red hair, violet would be just perfect. Then, of course, you have to have your reception near the water since Quinn was in the navy."

"Mom."

"I wonder what kind of cake we should get. I think four-tier is the perfect size. Vinnie's five-tier cake was ridiculous, and remember how it fell over."

"Mom!" I say again. "We're not getting married. That's not what I wanted to tell you about." I release a heavy breath. "I'm pregnant."

Quinn takes my hand in his, offering me support.

"You're what?" Dad asks.

"Quinn and I are expecting."

"But you told me about the"—her voice drops to a whisper—"baby without a man in the lab thing."

She clearly chickened out about telling my father about my plans because he looks like he might puke.

"Yes, but it turns out I didn't have to artificially inseminate myself because I was already inseminated—by Quinn."

My father doesn't move. His eyes shift, but nothing else does. They go back and forth between Quinn and me, deducing that I am not, in fact, the Virgin Mary and this wasn't an immaculate conception.

I wait for my father to be a dick to him.

Not because I don't love him and we're not happy, but because a bit of karma would be nice.

"Mr. Caputo," Quinn speaks, and my father's head jerks toward him. "I can assure you that I love Ashton. I want to be there for her, love her, and be a great father to our child. This wasn't what we planned to happen, but please know that it wasn't done out of disrespect."

"It wasn't respectful," I say under my breath. Quinn's hand squeezes, letting me know he heard me.

Quinn starts again. "I understand if you're angry, and I—"

Daddy's hand flies up, and I wait for him to backhand Quinn. That would be fine too.

"You two are back together, right?"

"Yes, sir."

"And you're having a baby together?" Dad asks again.

I answer. "We are."

He looks to my mother and then to us. "Okay then."

Okay then? "Okay . . ."

"Okay you're going to have a baby, and at some point, you're going to get married."

"Not any time soon," I clarify.

"Oh, it will be soon, my darling daughter. You have a few months to get your heads on straight before this baby comes."

I close my eyes and will myself to stay calm. "Daddy, when and if Quinn and I get married—"

"When," Quinn cuts in.

"*If*," I say for emphasis. "It will be on our terms. Right now, we're finding our legs in this entire relationship thing, so slow your roll on the marriage."

Mom is still clutching her chest. "But you're having a baby?"

I nod. "Yes."

Her smile widens, and her eyes fill with tears. "My baby is having a baby."

"Out of wedlock." I want to drive that home, but she doesn't seem to care.

She gets to her feet and comes around the table. "You'll have to go to confession about it because, right now, I'm just so happy."

Who knew my mother would like babies more than weddings?

chapter twenty-seven

QUINN

"**I**s Ashton with Natalie and Gretchen?" Mark asks, throwing his feet up on his desk.

"Yeah, she took a few days off so she could tell her friends about the baby."

He shakes his head. "Kids. I hope you're ready."

Liam said the same thing, and I'm starting to wonder what the hell we're in for, but it'll be fine because Ashton and I will figure it out.

The big hurdle of telling her parents is out of the way. They took it great, and I'm glad. I love her family. In the last few years, they've been better to me than my own. I called my mother last night and let her know on her voice mail. God only knows where she's living or if that is even her number anymore.

Our relationship is unsalvageable. She only calls me when she needs money. I never answer, and around and around we go.

I was more worried about telling my friends than her. Liam laughed, got me a beer, clapped me on the back, and told me to "be ready." Now, I'm getting the same sentiment from Mark, who is officially my boss.

God help me.

"I'm sure we'll figure it out."

"Let me give you some advice: let Ashton make all the choices. It's so much easier. Oh, did you guys decide on a wedding? I know a great minister."

"That was a mistake I witnessed firsthand, and I won't be making the same one," I say, cutting off that line of thinking.

Mark may be ordained, but he's not officiating my wedding. I'm happy to let Liam and Natalie be the only ones to know that joy.

"Suit yourself. Did you review the packet I emailed?"

I nod. "You'll want me here fifty percent of the time."

"At least. We haven't been doing a ton of protective details lately. We started to pull back after we realized that's where a lot of the issues were stemming from."

I lean back. "Yeah, you guys have had your share of bad luck."

"Thank God we've managed to avoid anything serious."

"Right. Still, have you gotten any closer to finding out where the leak and issues are coming from?"

Cole Security has had its share of bad luck. There is a breach that continues to cause issues. They thought they had it figured out when they found out who kidnapped Mark. Turns out, they weren't home free. As of late, they've had other things happening and hired Gretchen to come on and look over some of the legalities.

I'm now here to make sure there aren't any holes in the mission security, which was what Aaron was supposed to be doing.

Mark shakes his head. "We have our suspicions. Gretchen uncovered an issue with our legal team, but that guy was terminated and hasn't been seen since."

I feel for them. Mark and Jackson started this company as a way to handle their departure from the navy. Since then, they've hired other SEALs who the navy has discharged for mostly ridiculous reasons. To have to watch them constantly deal with that betrayal really sucks.

"What about Aaron?" I ask.

"What about him?"

"Where is he?"

For the last six months, he's been on an assignment for Cole Securities that no one talks about. Liam, Mark, Jackson, and Natalie are tight-lipped, even to me. When I asked Liam the other day, he said it was under control.

"He's fine," Mark says with a finality I know all too well. Mark and I held the same position when we were active. I've used that voice many times.

"Roger that."

That small response garners an inch of respect. I could push him, but it would be for nothing. This is his company and whatever I'm privy to is all I need to know.

"I appreciate that. I'd like you to take a look at the protective detail regulations. We wrote them a long ass time ago, and they need to be updated. Also, I'm going to have you create specs and battle plans, for lack of a better word, regarding each operation. I know we can't see all the possibilities, but right now, we are working with bare-bones regulations."

Because Aaron is gone and that was his job, which they failed to assign to anyone else.

I don't say it, but this is his specialty. I'm a sniper, not a strategist. Still, I know weak spots and how to avoid them.

"Not a problem. I'd like to do some weapons training with whoever is going to be assigned to me."

Mark grins. "I figured. You're approved for any training you deem necessary. Jackson and I have no problem spending money to keep our men trained."

"Good to know."

"Now, tell me about how you thought knocking Ashton up was the way to win her back."

I laugh once. "Wasn't the plan, but it seemed to work."

"Who knew the crazy redhead just wanted a baby?"

I did, and I'm damn glad I gave it to her.

"I love the beach," Ashton says as we walk through the surf, letting the small waves crash over our feet.

"You'd feel differently after going through BUDs."

She sighs as her head rests on my arm. "Maybe, but that's why I'm happy I studied biology instead of going through techniques to survive torture."

I laugh. That part wasn't fun, but yet, it kind of was. The things I learned may not apply to anything outside of what my job once was, but it's an experience that taught me that our bodies are stronger than our minds allow us to think.

Pain is a mindset, and if we can tackle that, we can push through it, which is what I'm trying to apply to all of my life.

"Since we're on the subject of jobs," I decide to broach the topic we've both been avoiding. "I think we should discuss what's going on here."

"You mean with you working for a company in Virginia Beach and me in New York?"

"Yes."

Ashton lifts her head and glances toward the sunset. I can't help but think about how absolutely gorgeous she is. The red and oranges in the sky make the blue in her eyes so much stronger. There's something about her that seems free and happy.

"I'm not sure what to say," she admits. "I don't know what we should do because I don't want to leave my job, and at the same time, it's not fair to ask you to live up there."

"I'll be able to be in New York at least fifty percent of the time."

She releases a heavy sigh. "So, that's like deployment each year? Six months of the year you'll be here and I'll be alone—with a baby."

In my head, this made much more sense. "It'll be broken up, so I won't be gone for months."

"No, I know that. It's going to be hard, though. Now that I had sort of hoped—"

"Hoped?"

Ash smiles bashfully. "I just hoped we'd be together. I don't know, I see us . . . raising this kid as a unit instead of me during the week and you on weekends."

Thank fucking God she said that.

I hesitate to ask this next thing. Ashton is headstrong, and if she feels her back is to the wall, she'll push back in ways I'd rather not see again. Right now, she's calm and relaxed, like a nice kitten. Those claws come out, and she's a freaking lioness. I like this version of cats.

Still, she wants us to talk and be able to say shit to each other, so here's a test.

"Can I ask you why moving here isn't even an option for you?"

Her fingers tense around my arm just a little. "It's not that it's not an option . . . is that what you want?"

"I don't want you to give up your life. I know your family and job are important."

"Yes, but Gretchen is here, and so are Natalie and Mark. I would have a family of sorts."

"And me."

She smiles at me and tilts her head. "Of course I have you."

Yes, she really does—by the balls.

"There's time for us to figure it out. I wanted to see where your head is."

Because my heart is with her. The idea of being here while she might need me there is weighing on me. I wish I could convince Mark and Jackson to open a New York office and let me run it, but that's ridiculous.

"Honestly, I'm conflicted in a way I never thought I would be." Ashton stops walking and stares out at the sea.

"How so?"

She looks up at me with those blue eyes from over her shoulder. "I've loved you for a long time, and six months ago, I never would've considered moving here. I would've stood my ground and demanded to stay in New York. Now, I don't feel like the ground is the same if you're not next to me."

We've said a lot to each other in the last few weeks. Confessions, apologies, and promises, but that might be the single most important thing she's said.

"What does that mean?"

She shrugs, takes my arms, and wraps them around her. "It means that I'm willing to consider going where you are if it means we can start our life together."

My lips brush the side of her head, and I place a kiss on her temple. "Fiery on the outside, sweet in the center."

She laughs and rests her head back, sinking into my embrace. "I'll show you fire."

"Don't make promises, *fragolina*."

God knows all that does is turn me on.

"Take me back to your apartment and let's see if we can burn it down."

I don't need her to say shit like that and not be willing to follow through. I scoop her up and start making my way off the beach.

"Quinn!"

"You said it, I'm just getting us there faster."

Her laughter fills the air as I move quicker, welcoming the burn.

chapter twenty-eight

ASHTON

"Well," Catherine bumps my hip as I stand here holding my niece, "you and Quinn are really happy?"

"We are. We're still working on the logistics, but the last month has been great."

I look at Erin Cole as I hold her in my arms and imagine what my child will be like. Will she or he be as tiny as this little one? Will they make the cute little faces she does? Will my child nuzzle in my arms or will I get a screamer?

"Good. I'm happy for you."

I smile at my best friend. "And I'm happy for you. She's perfect."

"She needs a friend."

"I'm hoping I have a girl and they can grow up and be best friends like we are."

Catherine nods. "Me too!"

We both start to laugh, and then Jackson enters the room. His eyes are troubled, but he smiles anyway. "There are my girls."

"Oh, Muffin, I love you too," I joke back.

"I forgot it was a package deal when I married her."

Catherine snorts. "I don't know how you could forget."

"I'll do better to remember."

"You do that, Jackson," I tell him with a stern nod.

"The minister is ready to perform the baptism. My mother is driving everyone crazy with baby pictures of Reagan and me, and your mother is three sheets to the wind. It might be a good time to go out there."

I rock Erin in my arms, bouncing her gently. "Auntie Ashton is going to officially be your Godmother, which means I get to spoil you rotten."

"Like you wouldn't anyway?" Cat challenges.

"And like you won't with my baby?"

"Yes, but remember that payback is a bitch, so whatever you do to me, it's going to come back to you."

I will do well to keep that little piece of information to myself. The three of us exit the room and head to where Mark is standing with his wife, Charlie.

"Ahh, Big Red, I always knew we'd find a way to have a kid together."

He's so stupid. "Yes, it was destiny."

Mark approaches, kissing my cheek before touching the baby's head. "She's really perfect. She's one hundred percent Catherine."

"For real. If she was Jackson, I'd be worried."

"Seriously," Mark agrees.

Jackson's smile is all teeth. "I regret this."

"Well, too late for it now, Muff. Let's get this show on the road so we can eat the food that Mrs. C. has been raving about."

My mother is Catherine's second mom. Cat claimed her when we were little because my mom is the best. She bakes cookies, makes dinner, and always has a stocked pantry.

Looking back, it was a smart plan on my mom's part.

Since Cat's mother has had a rough few years, Mama Caputo helped with the event today—more like ran away with this entire thing. She probably did it because it has to do with church, and anything she can do to save my mortal soul is something she's up for.

Also, Catherine wanted the party afterward to be at the Italian place that's always booked, and guess who got it done? Mommy.

"You know, if you upset the Jersey people, they will make sure you don't eat," I tell Mark with a lift of my shoulder.

"Your mother loves me."

I grin. "My mother loves everyone until she doesn't."

Mark bursts out laughing. "I'm a mother magnet."

"And an idiot."

"Says the woman who is pregnant with Quinn's baby."

"Says the man who hired my baby daddy." I raise a brow, waiting for his next one.

He moves closer, his eyes are full of mischief. "I've missed you, Red."

I shake my head. "I've missed you too."

And I have. Mark is one of those guys who makes all things better. His entire demeanor is hard to resist.

"You two done?" Jackson asks.

"We are."

"Can we get my daughter to the front of the church now?"

"Ehh, sure." I laugh, but refuse to hand the little girl over to her father as the four of us head up the aisle.

When we get to the front, I hold this precious little baby in my arms, grateful that I am a part of this while my own child is safely cocooned inside. I'm a little over three months along, and so far, she's already been to a wedding and now a christening. Though, I'd rather not make this a hat trick, so we can skip the funeral.

Erin is surrounded by her family and friends, who are also her family. Quinn sits in the front row with Charlie, Gretchen, Ben, Natalie, and Liam. His eyes stay on mine, and I see so much love I could cry. I watch as Quinn's gaze moves down to my belly where, thanks to this dress, you can see that I have a little bump.

At first, I thought I would hate the idea of being fat, but when that little bump became visible right before Gretchen's wedding two weeks ago, I decided I couldn't wait to get bigger. Quinn couldn't make it to the wedding since he had to take care of something for work. I was pissed, but then I was grateful he wasn't gone for longer than a few days.

"And do you promise to help guide the child through Christ?" the minister asks.

"Yes," Mark and I both answer in unison.

Just like that, she's baptized.

Everyone hugs, and Erin is placed back into her mother's arms. Quinn heads right toward me. "You okay?"

He's so overprotective, it's nuts. I hope we have a boy because, if it's a girl, he may end up building an ivory tower to stick her in. "I'm fine." His hand goes to my belly, and I feel his warmth through the dress. "The baby is fine too."

"Can you feel it?"

"No." I laugh. "We're way too early for that. I'm just saying it for your benefit."

"Oh, well, okay then."

He's been really cute. After Gretchen's wedding, I took a leave of absence from work because I needed to figure out where we'll end up. I have about five months of sick and vacation time saved, and once that runs out, I'll hopefully have a better plan.

"Soon we'll be there, though."

"I'm excited for it."

I don't know why it took an explosion to literally rock his

world, but Quinn isn't the same. Since being out of the navy, there's a calmness to him. He's still excited about us and the baby, but he smiles more. He's not worried about leaving, and I hope he's content.

The last thing I want is for him to feel suffocated.

"You seem happy," I tell him while touching his cheek.

"I am."

"Do you miss the military?"

Quinn shrugs. "I miss some of the guys on my team, but I'm getting to work with a new team." He hooks his arm around my shoulders, and we start to walk out of the church.

"Well, happy looks good on you," I tell him.

"You looked beautiful with a baby in your arms," Quinn says and then kisses my temple.

"Yeah?"

"Yeah."

It felt good. I held Erin, and everything inside me settled. It's everything I've wanted and now I'm going to have it . . . with a man I love. It seems like the world is smiling down on me.

"So"—Natalie grabs my hand—"you guys seem like you're doing great."

"We are."

"Quinn has changed, Ash. I see it in him, and I'm so happy."

I smile and lean back, sipping my water. "He really has. I keep wondering if maybe he regrets having a sort of instant family, but he has taken to living with me and preparing for a kid."

She nods. "He's definitely shocked Liam and me. I waited for a freak-out or something, but he just talks about how ready he is."

"Was Liam that way?"

Natalie looks over at him, her eyes turn wistful. "Liam is one in a million, but he's not without fault. When we got together, we had so much shit to overcome. I was married to his best friend, for one, and we thought Aaron was dead, so we were both grieving."

"I can't imagine."

"It was hard and I worried because Liam walked into an already established family. Aarabelle was a baby, and at the same time, it was as if he were competing with the ghost of Aaron. He stuck it out, though, and Quinn looks at you the same way that Liam would stare at me."

"I worry there are ghosts in his past too. With his shit family his trauma from serving, all these changes have to be hard on him. I mean he ended his career with the navy not even a few weeks ago and now he has a baby on the way. I don't know . . ."

These are things I've worried about but haven't given a voice to. He's been so happy, that I didn't want to jinx it. There are these moments, though. Times when he looks a little lost in New York. When he's working and focused on a task—he comes alive.

More than ever, I think I need to prepare to make the move to Virginia Beach. He's given up so much for me, and I want to show him that I'm just as devoted to making this work as he is.

"They all have things in their past," Natalie says softly. "Losing friends the way they have changed them. It's not something that you'll ever get used to seeing."

"It couldn't have been easy."

Quinn hasn't said much since the night he explained a very small amount of what happened. He doesn't talk about King or the guys who were in the accident. I haven't pushed. Maybe it's because things have been so good, and the last thing I want to do is screw that up.

"No, it's never easy for any of them, but I'm glad he woke up and saw what he had in front of him before it was too late," Natalie says with a smile. "I love Quinn like a brother. Not to mention he and Liam are thick as thieves, but I've always wanted more for him. I guess it's because I have everything I could've ever wanted and hope for the same for all the boys."

Natalie's relationship with Liam has always been something I've coveted. He's truly one of the best men I know. The way he came in and loved her child, respected her, and was willing to give her up if that was what she needed . . . I envied it.

"Did you . . ." I don't know if I should ask her this.

"Did I?"

"It's nothing."

Natalie rests her hand on my arm. "Ashton, you're my friend too. You can ask me anything."

This woman is a saint. "Did you ever worry that Liam would miss the single life?"

Liam isn't who I'm talking about, but I can't bring myself to say it. Quinn and I were dating in an unconventional way. While I think we were exclusive, I can't really know, and I've never asked. He went out, drank and partied, and if he did hook up, I never knew. It worked for us. I know I didn't step out on him. I loved him.

I wanted a future, but I'm not the girl who gets upset over things I can't control. This time, it's not that. He talks about marriage and raising our child together. It's not random or a shallow relationship.

There's a future.

"I think that *Liam*," her voice emphasizes that she knows who I'm referring to, "knows what he has. If he was ever going to miss being single, it wouldn't have been after major life decisions. You know, like if we had gotten pregnant or something along those lines."

I shake my head and touch my stomach. "I don't want the baby to be the only reason."

"Ash, he came back before the baby."

"I know."

"Do you?" She challenges.

I nod. "I do. It's just the first time I've ever felt comfortable, if that makes sense."

"So much sense. I remember when I was with Liam and thinking, is this what this is supposed to feel like? Was I actually living before? When you let yourself breathe because you're able to, it's really hard."

Our attention turns to where the guys are sitting. All of them are in some deep conversation. "What do you think they're talking about?"

She laughs. "Football. They only look that serious when they're arguing about sports."

"Men."

Natalie nods. "Exactly. But we love them. God knows why."

Because they make us smile. That's why.

chapter twenty-nine

QUINN

"That doesn't make sense," Mark chimes in. "I was the retribution for the shooting when we were all active. There's no one else who could be behind all this shit."

None of it makes sense. When I started looking into what Gretchen uncovered, it seemed as if the lawyer could've had something to do with the issues that keep happening, but I'm not so sure. I think he fucked up, but it doesn't seem like sabotage. It looks more like he was an idiot.

"Then why does it keep happening?" Liam asks. "I'm sorry, guys, but there's something else that you two aren't seeing."

"He's right. It's all around you guys." I look to Jackson and Mark. "Why else?"

Liam nods. "Maybe it has to do with something that happened before any of our time."

It's the only thing that would make any sense. "What missions did you guys go on where things went wrong?"

Mark bristles in his seat, but Jackson clamps his hand on his shoulder and then speaks. "We were in the heart of the war. Our team was first in, and we uncovered shit you guys can't begin to know. It could be anything. We were a part of raids where we seized assets that were . . ." He closes his eyes, seeming to go back in time. "Look, I know guys in our units took shit, I'm sure of it, but I never caught anyone."

"Not to mention, Jackson and I were the two dickheads who volunteered to keep extending. We worked with our team and also bounced to other units when they needed ops help."

Liam releases a heavy sigh. "I know this isn't easy, but there's a vendetta somewhere, and it's coming back in full force."

"It's only ever your protection details, right?" I ask.

"I wish." Jackson gets to his feet. "We've had issues with shipments and things going missing."

"I see." The worry is wearing on him. Anyone can see it. Jackson takes duty very seriously. He feels personally responsible for everything.

"The thing is, we go a fucking year with nothing, and then"—Mark claps his hands together—"we're right back here. It's like a goddamn game."

"One that almost killed you," Charlie materializes as if she was there the whole time.

Charlie is the only female in the world I wouldn't fuck with. She's a former CIA operative, and I'm pretty sure she still does some shit that we don't know about.

"I heard you that time," Mark says with a smirk.

"No you didn't, but I expect your hearing to continue to deteriorate with age," she digs at him.

They're so much like Ashton and me that it's funny. Well, minus the kicking the shit out of each other for fun. Each time, Charlie gives him a run for his money, and I'm pretty sure she lets him win so she doesn't hurt his ego.

"Watch it," he warns.

"Seriously, you guys are missing something. I've done what I can to get some answers, but whoever it is, they're hiding their tracks. I would go back as far as you can, figure out who you might've pissed off or who would be out for revenge," Charlie suggests. "None of the stuff leaked is of any consequence, it could be anyone. The information isn't secretive . . . it's just annoying. Think back. Think back to *who* would want to make things difficult for you."

"You know we've already done it," Jackson says. "We've gone over everything already and keep coming up with nothing."

"There's still one that I'm not sure about, Muff."

Jackson shakes his head with a half laugh. "No. It's not even a real option."

"What's not?" I ask.

Jackson grips the back of his neck. "I was married before. I ran Raven Cosmetics for a long time in my ex-wife's memory. Then, before I expanded to the California office, I sold my shares. Mark," he says his name like a curse, "seems to think Madelyn's family holds a grudge."

"It would make sense," Liam adds.

"Why? We all moved on a long time ago. I sold the company back to them, and her brother and I made amends over her death. It would make more sense if it was tied to the military."

The one thing I've learned about so many of these situations is that it actually doesn't ever make sense. Nothing we believe to be true is ever there. Irrational people aren't about sense and rational people don't tend to do shit like this.

"I don't know. I'm with Jackson," I speak up. "If they wanted to fuck with Jackson, they could've."

Mark shrugs. "But there were never any issues with Raven Cosmetics, only Cole Securities. If it was against Jackson, then wouldn't they want to hit him from all sides? But they didn't, which means that there was a personal reason that Raven wasn't touched. Don't you think that's odd?"

"You're what's odd," Jackson says with anger clear in his voice. "It's not my former in-laws."

"There's only one way to be sure." I get to my feet. "You need to look into it. You need to be sure because, if it isn't them, then you're back at zero."

"And how exactly do you think I'm going to do that? They know Mark and me."

I shrug. "They don't know me."

Jackson's eyes narrow, and Mark nods slowly. "He's right, Jackson. Quinn can go, snoop around, maybe gain access to people in their lives, and see if there's something fishy."

"And how is he going to do that?"

Please, like that wasn't what we did half the time we were on missions? "I tail him. I watch, and if I can get close enough, I can plant a device on them and listen. You know, all the shit we were trained to do."

I can see the uncomfortableness in Jackson's stance. "I don't like this. If they found out . . ."

"No one will know," I vow.

"I would." Jackson's voice is steel.

"I won't let anyone know who I am, Muffin."

He takes a few breaths. "Fine. They're in New York anyway. Consider this your first covert assignment. Don't fuck this up, Quinn."

I would laugh at him, but I have a feeling he might deck me. "Don't worry, I won't."

"So, you're investigating who is possibly sabotaging his company?" Ashton asks as she paces the living room.

I should've kept my damn mouth shut, but she asked why

I was wearing a suit. Usually, when we're in New York, I'm on the computer or video conferencing. I don't have to dress up, so when I came out today, she asked a million questions.

"I'm helping because they don't know me, so there is no reason for them to think Jackson is involved."

Ashton laughs with a roll of her eyes. "You're so stupid. You look like a cop or military. You don't think they'll be able to figure it out."

She has no faith in me sometimes. "I was trained to blend, Ash. Give me a little credit."

I can tell she's unhappy about this, but I thought she'd understand. We're in New York, and now I can stay for a few more weeks. Ashton is working at the lab for a few days this week and next because there's some case she wants to be involved in, so this should've been a happy thing.

"I'm not sure I'm okay with this."

"Okay with what?" I ask with my brows raised.

"You spying on some random people. How is this what you signed on for? You said you were going to be dealing with the logistics and security measures, not spying on his former in-laws."

"It's probably not even them."

"Then you probably shouldn't be doing this. It's fucked up and what's even more fucked up is that you're the one going! Why doesn't Jackson just ask them?"

I look at my watch, knowing that my schedule is tight. "I love you, Ash. I really do, but I have to go."

She rushes over to the door, crossing her arms over her chest. "I'm not moving." It's cute that she doesn't think I'll lift her and move her to the side.

"Ashton."

"Quinn. I'm going to give Jackson a piece of my mind about this."

No, she's not. I'm not playing a game with her. "I don't meddle in your work, you're not going to do it in mine."

She scowls at me, and huffs. If I weren't running late, I might find it adorable, but I am late, and right now, she needs to move aside. "Fine. I'm so mad though."

"You're being overly dramatic."

That was probably not the right thing to say.

Her eyes widen and her teeth clamp down. I swear her head is about to explode with how heavy she's breathing. I need to walk this back—quickly. "I didn't mean it like that. Just that the hormones are probably not helping, and you know what my job is. You know who I am."

A smile spreads across her face, and she moves toward the chair. Slowly, Ashton sits, her eyes watch me and I know I'm in for it. "You're right, honey. The hormones are making me dramatic."

I don't trust this. "Ash."

"No, no, I get it. I wouldn't want to worry about you. It's not like you're untrained."

"I'm not saying you don't have cause for concern."

She puts her hand up. "I won't even think about it again. I mean, why should I care that you're stepping into a possibly dangerous situation when we're finally on solid ground, right? There's clearly nothing to be uneasy about because, you know, people have only been blown up, shot, kidnapped . . . it's fine."

Fucking hell. I put my foot in my mouth this time. I crouch, taking her hands in mine. "I've never had anyone who worried about me when I left." Her blue eyes lift to mine. "I spent my entire military career not even bothering to tell anyone when I was gone or came back. This is new for me, *fragolina*. Yes, I had you for a few years, but you never cried when I left, did you?"

She nods. "I just never told you."

My heart breaks. I feel my chest grow tighter thinking of her being sad when I was gone. I didn't think about how she might have felt, and I fucking hate myself. "You cried?"

"I missed you, Quinn. I love you, and when you were gone, of course I worried and cried."

Jesus Christ. How dumb am I? I don't think there are even words to adequately describe what a fucking fool I was. I assumed she went on with her life as though I meant nothing. It was probably my own idiot way of coping too.

"I'm so sorry."

She touches her hand on my face. "You're making it hard to be angry with you."

"You have nothing to worry about, *fragolina*." I lean up and press my lips to hers. "I'm just going to observe, and I'll keep my distance unless I think there's something more. Jackson doesn't think it's them."

"This whole thing is unsettling."

I agree with her, but I don't want her to concern herself with any of this. I've been trained in ways she can't even imagine, and the last thing I'm going to do is be stupid. If it is Jackson's former in-laws, then they're using someone else to do it, and that's who I need to find. My plan is to find out what I can from afar and only get close if I have to.

"I trust Jackson," I tell her with conviction. "He wouldn't knowingly let any of his men walk into a dangerous situation. He'd do this himself, but he doesn't want to worry Catherine, and he doesn't think they're capable of any of this."

Ashton releases a heavy sigh. "You know she'll kill him if she finds any of this out."

"Not my problem."

She leans in, kissing me softly. "No, but I'll be your problem."

"You're my favorite problem to have."

Fire ignites in Ashton's eyes. "And what exactly would you do with me, Mr. Miller?"

The sheer number of things I'd like to do with her are staggering. "First," my voice drops. "I'd like to kiss you."

"I like that." She smiles against my lips. "What else?"

"Take every fucking thing you're wearing off."

My cock goes hard as I imagine her naked. It's only been twelve hours since I had her, but I want her again. Hell, I want her all the time. If I could get a job where all I do is pleasure her, I'd work overtime.

"I'm liking this problem-solving."

I grin, pull her to her feet, and wrap my arms around her. "Then wait till you see the rest of my plans."

I'm thinking we have a lot of things to work out, so I should get busy. Then I bring my lips to hers and get very, very busy.

chapter thirty

ASHTON

"So, why is this so important to you?" Quinn asks while I practically drag him toward the boardwalk.

"Well, you are about to experience what should be a staple in every person's life."

"Eating a cheesesteak?"

I shake my head with an exasperated sigh. "This isn't just *any* cheesesteak, this is a Midway cheesesteak, Quinn. It's where all the magic happened for North Jersey girls."

My summer didn't begin until I had one of these. Catherine, Gretchen, and I would drive to Seaside Height at the first sign of warmth for one of these. This beach is the beach of my youth. Now, if Quinn is going to be an active participant in my future, he must experience all the things that make me—me.

"I'm not a North Jersey girl, babe."

"No, but you're having a baby with one."

"So, we drove over two hours for a sandwich?"

I groan and tug harder. "Just go in with an open mind."

We walk up the steps, and the sea air hits me. It's home. There hasn't been a single summer since I turned sixteen where I didn't come here. When Gretchen got her license, we would

drive here each weekend. Our parents hated it, but it was free-
dom for us.

There was nothing like a Friday night, windows down, blar-
ing some Nelly, and sitting in bumper-to-bumper traffic on the
parkway.

Every car was filled to the brim with teenagers, trying to
escape to the shore.

And that's not even mentioning prom weekend. I look over
to the right, knowing the hotel that's one block off the beach is
where I lost my virginity. I should probably leave that part out
when selling my love for the shore.

"I'm still not understanding why going to the beach was
necessary for you. New York City is on an island."

"It's down the shore. *Down the shore*, not the beach, not the
ocean, not going to catch waves . . . learn the lingo," I chide as
we move forward. "Sheesh, people will think we're tourists."

Quinn's gaze sweeps the horizon, and I wonder if he's seeing it the way I do. The hurricane destroyed this place and then
a fire destroyed it even more. The old roller coaster that was on
the pier was sitting in the ocean after Hurricane Sandy. I remember watching the television, calling Cat, and both of us crying.
My cousin's beach house was completely flooded, and so many
people we know lost everything.

But no matter what people say about New Jersey . . . the
people who live there are strong and don't surrender.

We fight.

So, while it's not the same roller coaster, there is a new one.
And even though I didn't kiss my high school boyfriend at the
top of that one, I'd bet another girl has, which makes me smile.

"There are actual boards," he muses as he kicks the ground.

"Yes, which is why it's called a boardwalk, unlike in Virginia
where you have it paved."

"We pave it so people don't trip, like that guy . . ."

Silly Quinn. "That's part of the experience."

He wraps his arm around my shoulders, pulling me to him and then kisses the top of my head. "Sometimes, I wonder about you."

"Wonder away, but wait until you officially become Jersey approved."

He doesn't seem all that excited, but he will be.

We walk a bit and then the stand comes into view. In the middle of the boardwalk, there it is . . . Midway Steak House.

"That is where you wanted me to eat? It looks like a carnival stand."

Oh, no. He will not ruin my day at the shore. I know that he's overly careful about what he eats, but I'm not having it. We are going to enjoy this as though calories don't count.

I turn to him, making sure my voice is strong and convincing. "For one day, you're going to indulge me. You're going to eat fatty, greasy foods, and like it. You'll get ice cream wrapped in a waffle, fries, a cheesesteak, and maybe even some cotton candy because I'm pregnant and you did it to me."

"On one condition."

"I don't think you're in the position to bargain."

Quinn grins as his hands rest on my hips. "I'm pretty sure you love me and I'm not going anywhere. So, now that we've established my groveling period is officially over, I'm most definitely in the position I want to be in."

"Are you so sure of that?" I ask with one eyebrow raised.

"Yup."

Damn it. He's right. I do love him and I'm not about to get rid of him—even if it's over food.

"What are your demands?"

He fights back a smile, but I still see it before he is able to control himself. "First, after this, you're going to clean up your diet. You need to eat better, especially since you're eating for two."

I look at my belly with a frown. "The baby likes fries."

"The baby"—he shakes his head—"should eat more apples than fries."

"Whatever."

"Second, you and all fast food are about to break up." I go to open my mouth, but he starts back up before I can speak. "I know that you like it and I know the baby likes it, but if you want a day of me eating food I would never touch, then you're going to sacrifice a bit for me."

"For how long?

"One week."

That's not even an option. "No way. One day for you and one week for me?"

"Fine, two days."

He's nuts. I'm not giving up junk food because of this. Then I think about how I should turn the tables on him. Quinn wants me to quit junk food because he's a health nut? Well, he hasn't seen me really eat because I often hide some of it around him. "You know . . ." I say sweetly. "I was thinking, and you're right."

"I am?"

"Yeah, you shouldn't have to eat anything you don't want, even if it is something I want to share with you." Quinn's eyes narrow. He knows I'm up to something. I drop my head, looking at where my hands rest on his chest. Very innocently, which is not innocent at all, I start to move my fingers as though I'm playing with the fabric. "I know that it's important to you to stay healthy, right?"

"Ash?"

Very slowly, I raise my head and look at him through my lashes before our eyes are fully engaged. "I'm sorry. I was being selfish wanting to give you a little part of my past. You see, if we had gone to school together, I'm one hundred percent sure it would've been *us* eating a cheesesteak and not my ex-boyfriend."

His hands tense. Yeah, he's done for. The one thing that Quinn can't handle is me thinking about another man, even if said event happened before his time. "If it means that much . . ."

"No, no," I say quickly. "There's so much that I did here, and I wanted to have you be the man who erased the old memories and replaced them with new ones."

"Memories?"

"Yeah, I mean, my ex-boyfriend in high school used to bring me here for a cheesesteak and then we'd ride the rides, get cotton candy, and he'd play a game until he won something." Which he never did because he was cheap, but I don't tell him that.

"Oh."

"Yeah, and then in college, this guy I was seeing would bring me here on the weekends sometimes, and we would get an ice cream waffle. I just . . . I want to have that with *you*." He seems to be at a loss, and I use this moment to go for the kill. "I'm sorry, Quinn. I just love you."

"Don't be sorry. I didn't know, and I would erase your entire past if I could, sweetheart." He leans forward, bringing his lips to mine.

"Come on, let's go get that cheesesteak."

Life with him is going to be so fun if I get my way this easily.

"You are not riding a damn roller coaster. I don't give a shit what memories you have on it, you're pregnant."

As if I didn't know that. "I didn't say I wanted to. I was explaining that it had sentimental value."

Quinn's posture relaxes now that he sees he won't have to fight me. Our day has been the best. I'm so glad I coerced him into bringing me here and away from work, where he's still spying for two idiots named Mark and Jackson.

"Can we at least ride the carousel?" He looks like he's ready to throw himself off the pier. "Please," I whine.

"I'm totally getting a blow job tonight."

I'll agree to anything if I can stay here a little longer. "Fine."

"I don't believe you."

I shrug. "Let me ride the pony, and then I'll ride you."

He groans, his head falling back. "If you take one photo of this, I swear . . ."

Oh, the temptation is strong with that one. How much fun would it be for the guys to see him straddling a freaking plastic horse? The blackmail that I would be in possession of is almost worth it. However, he's given me the best day ever.

Everything I wanted to do, we've done. Games, the arcade, the food—hell, even walking on the boardwalk with him was the best.

Almost as good as our date in New York. The only reason it doesn't top that is because that was our first real date, and it will always be my favorite.

This is a very close second.

"I promise no photos. I have this entire day cataloged in my head."

Quinn's lips touch my forehead. "Then let's go make sure you never forget it."

We get our tickets to ride and get on right away. It's a little later in the season, and since it's a weekday, it's not nearly as crammed. "I want the one with pink hair."

He runs his hand down his face. "And here I thought you might try to emasculate me and make me take it."

"I would never. You can ride the black stallion."

"Yes, that makes it all better."

I ignore his comment and climb up. "This is so great!"

Quinn getting on the horse is pure comedy. He's big and the seat isn't so he's sitting half ass on and half on the back.

Do not take a photo, Ashton.

I swear I will be a grown-up.

"You know, this carousel has been around since like 1930."

"They must've been smaller men back then," he notes.

Before either of us can say more, the ride begins. Slowly, we turn, the horse going up and down gracefully. I hold on to the pole and look up, watching the mechanisms go before I close my eyes and smile.

When I pull myself back, I look to the man I love. He's sitting there, staring at me with the strangest expression. "What?"

"You."

"Me?"

Quinn nods. "You're beautiful, and when you were holding on, head back, and smiling . . . it took my breath away."

Now it's my turn to struggle to breathe.

His hand extends, and I don't hesitate placing mine in his. We ride for the rest of the time with our fingers intertwined, enjoying the moment.

The ride stops, Quinn dismounts and comes to help me off. We stand there, facing each other, and my heart races. I don't know why, but I feel as though everything has changed in this last few moments.

"Thank you," I say as my hand lifts to touch his cheek.

"No, my sweet *fragolina*. Thank you. I don't know what I would do if we never had a day like this."

"Me either, and I'm glad we never have to know."

He leans in, giving me the sweetest kiss. "No, we never will know a life without each other because I will never let you go. Ever."

chapter thirty-one

ASHTON

"I'M SO TIRED," I COMPLAIN AS QUINN KISSES MY FOREHEAD. All week, he's been following around Jackson's former in-laws. Last night, he didn't get home until after eleven, and since becoming pregnant, I'm ninety years old and can't stay up that late anymore.

"Go back to sleep, love."

"I can't now. I'm up," I grumble as I reach for him. I'd much rather he stay in bed. "Come back here."

"I have to work."

"You mean stalk."

Quinn sits on the bed beside me, pushing my hair back off my face. "You feel warm."

"It's because I'm hot for you," I mutter with one eye open.

He smiles. "Are you feeling okay?"

I swat his hand away. "I'm fine. I'm tired and cranky since you suck and won't stay in bed with me."

I wanted a snuggle day. I never thought I'd be the kind of girl who would want to lie around with a guy because I love work. It gives me purpose and joy, but after taking a few weeks off, I realize this is the good life. Maybe I was built to be a trophy wife, who knew?

"I'm serious, are you getting sick?"

I lean up and glare at him. "No, I'm hot when I sleep. I feel fine."

"Okay. Well, I would've stayed with you if you were sick."

Asshole.

I fake cough. "Come to think of it . . . I am feeling a little congested."

He gets to his feet with a laugh. "Nice try, babe. I'll be back early. I just need to check on something."

So he says now. "Whatever."

I flop back onto the bed as he walks out the room. I hear the front door click and curl on my side, hoping to fall asleep.

I end up staring at the door to the bathroom, when I would much rather be looking at my hunky boyfriend, and get pissy. Not wanting to let my mood take over, I rise and start to clean my apartment. The one thing that Quinn does that makes me crazy is refuse to put anything in a hamper.

Why is this so hard?

You bend down, pick it up, and put it in the basket. The man can dismantle a gun with his eyes closed but can't manage this. It's maddening.

I grab his socks, which were tossed haphazardly on the floor. Then I grab his shirt, which apparently couldn't make it there either. And finally, I snatch up his pants, which were under the shirt.

Seriously. I'm going to beat him.

I gather the laundry and head to the machine. There are some people who hate to clean, but I love it. It's a perfunctory task that allows me to give order to an otherwise chaotic world. I sort the clothes and then start to fill the tub. I empty the pockets of each item and when my hand hits something hard, I groan.

"Quinn."

I pull out the object and my heart drops. It's a ring box. A black, velvety ring box. It might not be *that* kind of ring. He's given me a ring actually. It sits on my right ring finger, reminding me that he loves me without end.

A good person would put the box back, not look, and go on with their life. I've never once claimed to be good.

What do I do?

I grab my phone and video chat Catherine.

"Hey." She smiles as she comes on screen. Erin is resting on her chest, head nestled into the crook of her neck.

"Awww. She's so cute."

"She didn't sleep at all last night."

"Yeah, you look like shit," I say with the love only a best friend has.

"Thanks."

"So . . ." I go right into it. "I was doing the laundry, and I found something."

Catherine's eyes alight with interest. "Do tell . . ."

I lift the black box and show it to her. "Do you think . . .?"

"Open it!" she whisper-shouts.

See, this is why I call her for stuff like this. Gretchen would've scolded me and given me shit about ruining a surprise. She's the friend that we would call *after* we buried the body. Catherine is who helps dig the hole.

I position the phone so she can watch and lift the lid.

Sure enough, it's *that* kind of ring.

"Holy shit," we both say in unison.

It's beautiful. It's insanely perfect and . . . it's huge. There sits what has to be at least a two-and-a-half-carat, princess-cut solitaire. I pull it out, holding it up and inspecting it. "How much is Jackson paying him?" I ask.

"Wow, Ash. That's gorgeous. He did good."

Yeah he did. "I don't know what to say now."

"What do you mean?"

"How the hell do I talk to him knowing he has this sitting around for whenever?"

Catherine groans. "You cannot ruin this for him."

"Of course I can't, but I will! I'm impatient as fuck on a good day, but now? Knowing that this is here? I'm screwed!"

I didn't think this through at all. I wanted to know if it was a ring, I didn't fret over what the hell I would do if it was one. Shit.

I don't know how to process this.

Quinn is serious about all his marriage talk. He has a freaking ring. I try to rack my brain to figure out if he mentioned anything special coming soon. I don't think there are plans. All he's been doing is following around Jackson's possible suspect, which Catherine doesn't know about. At least I can keep that secret.

We don't usually keep secrets from her, and this is one I really hate. She should know about his company issues. Hell, once upon a time, she was hired to actually handle the issues he was facing. Catherine is a damn publicist and crisis management something or other. She's smart with this stuff, but *nooo*, these idiots want to make sure she thinks things are good.

"Ashton," Catherine calls my name.

"Huh?"

"What the hell is going on in your mind?"

I can't tell her that. "Scary things, my friend."

"Well, that wouldn't be unusual."

"Sad, but true. How do I get him to propose tonight?"

Catherine's eyes close, and she is clearly gathering her wits. I tend to get this reaction from her often. "You can't push him on this. I know you think it's fine, but it's not. He needs to give it to you when he's ready."

I let out a loud groan. "I hate you."

"I'm used to it."

I collapse onto the couch and a wave of nausea hits me. I don't know if it's nerves or something else, but I feel like shit. My hand sits on my stomach, and my face scrunches up.

"You okay?" Cat asks.

"Yeah, I just don't feel . . . right."

"That's called having a conscience. The feeling will pass once you get used to it."

"You know, I don't like you all that much right now."

She ignores that because it's not like she hasn't heard it before. Another roil goes through me, and I sit up in case I'm going to hurl. It doesn't seem like that's the issue, though. It's a slight cramp.

"Did you eat something bad?"

I shake my head. "No, I don't think so, and aren't I a bit late for morning sickness? But it's almost like a little cramp in my side."

Catherine nods with a worried look on her face. "I had a bit of cramping when Erin was growing. My doctor said it was normal."

"It is? I don't know. Maybe I need to lie down. Between Quinn being out all day, the ring, and everything else, I'm . . . I'm just out of it."

"Sounds good, go put the ring away first and then get some rest. Call me when you wake up so I don't worry, okay?"

I agree, and we hang up. I do as she says, then throw yesterday's outfit back onto the floor the way he had it—or, at least the best I can remember, and curl back into bed. Another cramping feeling comes on, and I take a few deep breaths.

I try not to let my mind go too far over the deep end of doom. I'm fifteen weeks along which is more than I was when I lost the first baby. We've done everything right with doctor's appointments, and there's been nothing to indicate anything is wrong.

This could be nothing. Dinner last night could be sitting wrong. I could be getting sick like Quinn thought.

Yes, that's what it probably is.

A virus.

I close my eyes and put my meditation app on because I need some Zen and peace. When I wake up, it'll be fine.

chapter thirty-two

QUINN

WHAT SHOULD'VE BEEN NO MORE THAN AN HOUR HAS turned into three. Madelyn's father is a strange guy. Thanks to Charlie's "friend," we were able to hack into his calendar. Today, he is meeting with someone.

Normally, an appointment wouldn't stand out. Hell, everyone meets someone, but it was the way it was labeled that caught our attention.

Now, I'm waiting at a coffee shop, trying to blend in as I watch him stare out through the windows.

His demeanor is what has my senses sharpened. He's fidgeting—a lot.

My phone rings in my pocket, and I see Ashton's face.

I debate answering, but then I remember how she was before I left. "Hey," I say turning my head so no one will be able to see me.

"Hey, where are you? Are you on your way yet?"

She sounds fine, and I breathe a sigh of relief. "I'll be home soon."

I wish I were heading back to her now. I have a big plan for us for after I scope out this meeting. We are going to walk through

Central Park again, enjoy the nicer weather since it'll be getting colder soon. Then I'm going to take her to dinner, which is where I'm going to ask her to marry me.

"Okay, but I'd like you to come home."

"I can't right now, but I promise, I'd much rather be with you."

She sighs. "How long do you think?"

I smile because, a few months ago, she wouldn't have asked when I was coming home, she'd be trying to knee me in the balls. Everything has changed, and all because of one moment in time. It's sad to think about how, if that hadn't happened, I wouldn't be here—not in this shop, I'd rather not be here, but in my life—right now. I have the love of a woman I don't deserve, a job that doesn't suck, and a baby on the way.

In about a month, we should find out if it's a boy or a girl, and then, god help my credit card, Ashton and I can start to plan more.

I want to convince her to move to Virginia. Our friends are there, and it would be good for us to get a fresh start away from the city.

"Maybe another half hour?"

"Okay, I'm . . . I'm not trying to be a pain, I'm just not feeling right. I tried to take a nap, but I can't sleep."

My pulse spikes, but I calm myself immediately. Fear is a mindset. "What doesn't feel right?" I ask and then turn to look for the subject, but he's gone.

Fuck.

"I don't know, I feel weird . . . and I'm probably being overly stupid, but I want you home."

"Okay, I'm on my way. Give me a few."

I can almost hear the relief when she says, "Thank you, babe. I'm sure it's fine. Really, I can wait a bit, just talking to you already made me feel better."

"Are you sure?"

"Yeah. I'll call my mom while I wait.

"I'll be there soon," I promise.

I make my way out of the coffee shop and look both ways, scanning the people until I spot the top of what I believe to be his head. I follow, staying two people behind just in case, and then stop when I see him talking to someone—a woman.

I continue on, mainly because this is the way home anyway, and observe. They turn the corner, and I debate what to do. I can follow him and see what the hell he's doing or go home to Ashton.

That gut feeling that something isn't normal is telling me this isn't nothing. People don't schedule meetings and move them for no reason.

I close my eyes for a split second and turn where he did. I need to follow this through. I won't be more than ten minutes.

I walk down the road, which isn't nearly as busy as the street we turned off. There's a small store and another coffee shop, so I do my best to look uninterested while taking it all in.

My gaze scans, but he's not around, and then I hear something coming from the parking garage to my right.

I move, staying close to the building as I duck inside and behind a pillar.

"It's not like that," the voice of Jackson's former father-in-law says.

A male voice laughs. "It's exactly like that. Pay up."

I move forward a little more, staying as close to the shadows as I can. "I paid you already. I don't know what else you could want."

The female speaks this time. "I'm sorry."

"It was one time, Jennica. One time that I slept with you, and you're making me pay for it for the rest of my life. My wife has been through enough and I won't have her hurt."

Someone is blackmailing them. It's clear, but for money? That's nothing to do with Jackson.

"I know, and I'm sorry. I promise I will never contact you again," Jennica says with a hint of sadness.

It's clear that Jennica is being used to get to Jackson's former father-in-law, but why? Either way, it's nothing to do with Cole. At least there's some relief there.

The man I've been following sighs. "Just, let me be. Don't come back again. There will be no more money."

Mistakes that come back to haunt us never really go away.

She goes quiet, and I hear footsteps heading my way. I slink even farther back, moving behind the pillar and off to the side.

He passes me, and a second later, the girl behind him follows. I wait until she rounds the corner, and my phone buzzes.

Ashton: Quinn, come home. Now. Something's wrong with the baby.

Fuck. No. I have to get the hell out of here and to her.

Moving quickly, I walk toward the exit of the garage, but before I get there, someone taps my shoulder.

I spin fast, instantly regretting that I forgot there was a third person.

Before I can register anything, something slams so hard into my head that everything goes black.

chapter thirty-three

ASHTON

OMETHING'S WRONG. SOMETHING'S VERY WRONG. TEARS ARE coming, and my blood pressure is through the roof. I can taste the adrenaline coursing through me.

I take a few breaths and look back at the couch where there's a few drops of blood where I was sitting.

Oh, God.

I can't.

This can't be happening again. I can't endure losing another child. Not one that I really want. Not *this* baby—our baby.

I grab my phone and shoot him a text.

Me: Quinn, I don't want to scare you, but I need you to come home now. Please call me.

My hands are shaking as I drop the phone. After a few minutes without a response, I start to feel sick. Where is he? He always answers me.

Maybe he's on the subway. When he resurfaces, he'll call.

In the meantime, I call Clara. She answers on her personal line, which I only have because I'm a friend.

"Ashton?"

"Clara, something's wrong. I felt some cramping."

"That can be perfectly normal," she tries to reassure me.

"Yes, but now I'm bleeding," I say the words as fresh tears fill my vision.

It's like déjà vu all over again. The cramping will worsen and then there will be no options.

I'll lose the baby. I'll lose Quinn. I'll be alone again.

"Okay, can you get into the city or would you rather go to the hospital in Brooklyn and I'll meet you there?"

"No, I can come there. It's probably nothing, but I'm. . . nervous."

Clara's voice is calm and soothing. "Take a deep breath, relax, and meet me here."

I nod. "I can't get a hold of Quinn and . . . I'm scared, Clara."

I'm so afraid this is going to be my life. I'll get pregnant and then my body will fail me. I'm just over fifteen weeks. This shouldn't be happening. We were smart and careful and we did everything right. I stopped working for fuck's sake. I'm not on my feet for too long. I always take care of myself.

"Okay, I want you to take a cab here. It could be nothing, Ashton. How much blood was it?"

"Not a lot. I mean, there was definitely blood."

"All right. Come in and I'll get you in immediately."

I try to control my breathing, but I feel as though my lungs are being ripped from my chest.

Staying calm has to be my priority. The more upset I get, the worse this will be. Somehow I manage to get a text out to Quinn.

Me: I'm trying to get a hold of you, but you're not answering. I'm heading to see Clara. Meet me there.

No response.

Me: Please just text me back. I'm starting to worry.

Still nothing.

I try some yoga breaths, hoping to relax enough to get myself to the office.

My legs feel uneasy as I make my way to the cab. I give him the address and then call Mark. Whatever Quinn was doing, he'd check in with him, right?

"Hey, Red."

"Mark, something's wrong. I'm going to the doctor now, but I can't find Quinn."

I don't have time to sugar coat anything, and while Mark may be a jackass, he would never joke when there's distress.

"Okay, when did you last talk to him?"

"I don't know, maybe a half hour ago. He said he was on his way but was working on something."

Mark's voice is deep and there's no playfulness now. "Let me track his location. He checked in from the coffee shop, but that was about a half hour ago." I chew on my thumbnail, feeling as if I could pass out at any moment. "It says he's at a parking garage, but . . ."

Dread fills me. "But what?"

"Nothing. Let me try him, but don't worry, Ash. Quinn is the best, I'm sure he just dropped his phone."

Quinn is the best, which means that he doesn't drop things like his phone. "Mark . . ."

"I'll call you back."

He doesn't want to tell me. I've been on the receiving end of a Mark Dixon call about bad news. I heard his voice when he told Catherine that Jackson was shot. I heard all about how he was the one who told Natalie about Aaron. Mark has been the bearer of bad news too many times.

When I thought about losing Quinn a little while ago, this wasn't what I was thinking.

My hand clutches my chest as I pray for the first time in a very long time, hoping my mother's efforts afford me a little good grace.

"Dear God, please let this baby be okay. Please don't let me lose another one, and please don't let anything be wrong with Quinn," I whisper each word as the cabbie drives over the bridge. "Please don't take everything I love in one day. I can't . . . I can't." A sob breaks from my chest, and I clasp my hand over my mouth, silently saying the rest because I can't say it aloud. *"I can't live through it."*

chapter thirty-four

QUINN

*F*UCKING HELL, MY HEAD. THAT'S THE ONLY THOUGHT THAT registers. Something hit me, and my head is throbbing. My hands go to move around, but they're bound.

What the fuck?

I try to gather my thoughts, but it hurts to think.

Hell, it hurts to think about thinking.

Slowly, I start to assemble a plan. First, figure out where I am.

Honing on my sense of touch, I use the little room I have with my fingers and feel what I can. It's cheap carpet. I move my feet, and when I push, my head slams into something hard and lights dance inside my eyelids. Jesus, I'm in a trunk of a car.

Okay, calm down and think.

I was following him, and we went to a garage. There were three people, and I saw two leave. How the fuck could I be so stupid?

Another few minutes go by, and my head hurts worse than anything I've ever felt before, which is saying something considering I went through an IED explosion. I try to get some kind of upper hand, working the knots on my wrist, but whoever tied these wasn't an amateur.

Once again, I refocus. What do I remember? A face? A voice? Anything familiar?

No.

I'm struggling to get my brain to connect any dots or pick out any clues, but there are none.

Nothing about this makes sense. Why the hell was I grabbed? No one should have known I was there unless someone was following me.

But who?

I scoot around, trying to feel if my phone is in my pocket, but they must have taken it. I had it in my hand . . . thinking about getting back to Ashton.

Ashton. She's never going to forgive me for this. She called me upset, and instead of going home to her, I followed the son of a bitch.

I start to berate myself, hating that whatever had her upset, I'm not there for. Of all the times I've failed her, this is one I'll regret most.

Before I can get too far in my head, I hear someone at the back.

"And what do you want to do with him?"

The voice is muffled.

"Just tie him up?"

Again the response is too low for me to hear the answer. They're either trying to hide themselves or are on the phone.

"Look, I'm not comfortable with all that . . ." The guy trails off, and I close my eyes to focus on the sounds around me. "I'll leave him for you then."

I revert back to my training. I need to leave my own head and focus only on the things I can control. I have to put Ashton out of my mind because she's the only thing that can break me. If I want to get back to her, I can't allow myself any mistakes.

The trunk flies open, and light spills in, making it impossible to see anything. A large man looms over me, he's so backlit that I can't make out a single feature on his face.

His hand lifts, and I feel the stab of a needle into my arm.

"What? No hello?" I manage to get out before my world goes black once again.

chapter thirty-five

ASHTON

M̵Y HANDS REST ON MY STOMACH AS WE MAKE OUR WAY through the traffic. My cab driver must sense my panic because he's been extra aggressive since we entered Manhattan. There's no control over my body right now. No amount of breathing can calm me.

Everything feels as if it's going in slow motion. Maybe this is a good thing because Quinn explained stressful situations as almost like fast forward. The fact that I can dissect each thought surely means it must not be as life-threatening, right?

I check my phone again for anything from Quinn, but nothing.

I close my eyes, and it rings.

Mark.

"Where is he?"

"I don't know yet. We're doing everything we can to find out. I have each member of my staff trying to track him, but he could've dropped his phone, Ash."

The thing is, in the depths of my heart, I don't think that's true. "Find him, Mark."

"I will. What's going on?"

I don't want to tell anyone before Quinn, but my breathing hastens and I start to hyperventilate. "I can't . . . I can't . . . breathe."

"Easy, Red. Easy. Listen to me, he'll be fine. Quinn is a smart guy, and he would never do anything stupid. Now, just breathe."

I try my best. He's right, Quinn is all of that, but he's not invincible. None of them are, regardless of what they think.

Another cramp hits, and I start to cry harder. "I'm losing everything."

"No. You're not losing anything. Where are you?"

"I am!" I cry out. "I'm going to lose the baby." I choke on the words.

"Ashton, you're just upset, okay? I know it's stressful, but you have to stay calm. Tell me where you are."

"In the cab."

On my way to find out if, once again, my body has failed me.

I hear him cover the phone but I know he's barking out orders to find me. Then another voice shouts back, and then the voice on the call isn't Mark's anymore.

"Ashton?" Natalie's says. "Are you bleeding?"

I nod with tears streaming. "There was a spot, but I . . . I don't know now."

"Okay. Are you on your way to the doctor?"

"Yes."

"Good. Is anyone with you?" Natalie's soothing tone puts me at ease, just slightly.

"No, I'm alone."

The line goes quiet for a moment, but then she's back, asking, "Is it the doctor you work for?"

"Yeah, and where the fuck is Quinn?"

Natalie understands more than anyone what I'm feeling. She went through hell with her first husband, and Liam has had a few moments that would turn anyone's hair gray.

"I know you're worried, but Mark, Jackson, Ben, and the rest of the guys are working on it."

My voice is trembling, and I try to get it under control. "I'm here. I have to go inside and . . . and pray."

"Trust me, Ashton, no one in this group is going to let this rest. We'll find Quinn and get him to you as soon as we can."

I believe her, so I put a bit of my faith in her words.

After exiting the cab, I can't help but look back at the seat and thank every God, angel, and my mother because I'm pretty sure she's a saint that there's no blood there.

Maybe it was nothing. Maybe it was some spotting like Clara said. Oh, I pray that's the truth.

Okay, I can do this. I just need to get some answers and figure out if there's anything wrong. For the first time, my chest doesn't feel as though someone is sitting on it, and I walk to the entrance of the clinic.

The door opens, but before I can cross the threshold, my stomach tightens, forcing me to grip the door so I don't fall to my knees.

chapter thirty-six

QUINN

TRY TO OPEN MY EYES, BUT I CAN'T. NO MATTER HOW HARD I attempt to engage the muscles, they won't budge. My body is heavy and everything feels murky.

The air around me is saturated with the scents of rust, dirt, and salt. I try to listen for any noises, but all I hear is the sound of running water. Which tells me I'm alone. I start to recount my training, stay calm, use what is available. At all costs, think through each action because the only control I have is reactions.

I was taken, hit over the head, and drugged. Clearly, someone is tied to Cole and knows who I am. Now, I need to figure out where I am so I can create a plan to get out of here.

There's the noise of a train which means I could still be in New York City, but I have no clue at this point. Hell, I don't even know how long it's been. Hours? Days? There's no way to tell, but I know I'm hungry, thirsty, and I could really use an Advil.

I move my neck side to side, cracking my jaw because the bastard who hit me definitely didn't hold back. This guy knew exactly where to hit to cause maximum damage, which wouldn't be Jackson's former in-laws.

Not to mention he had already left by the time I got clocked.

There's a noise outside of whatever room I'm in, but the tingling in my fingertips draws my attention. My arms aren't tied, and slowly, my limbs come back to me. I try to force my vision to return, but it's still no good. So, I work on what I can.

I lift my arm a bit before it falls back to my side, but that's progress.

I hear a low chuckle, and I instantly want vengeance. Whoever is sitting here is watching me, studying my movements, and I won't be making another mistake. He thinks I'm weak, which I only am thanks to the fucking drugs he gave me.

The next time I move, it'll be to slit his fucking throat.

I focus on my toes, which are still in my shoes. I move each one deliberately. Each time, the movement becomes more controlled.

Since I'm on my side, the next are my fingers. I curl them, one at a time, until I'm able to make a fist.

Good. At least whatever drugs they gave me are wearing off.

Now, I start to count. Time is the only measurement I can use to start to get a grip.

The next things I can control are the muscles in my legs. And as each moment passes, another piece comes back to me.

"He's waking up," the same guy from the car says.

Whoever he's talking to agrees without a word, just a slow hum.

"Should we knock him out again?"

Again with only a sound, indicating he doesn't want to do it.

This guy is going out of his way to keep his identity concealed. Slowly, I crack an eyelid open. If I know who I'm dealing with, I can get my ass out of here and back to Ashton.

As soon as I do, something moves, blocking my view. "He said you would do this. You'd start to gather your wits and then you'd try to see. You're inventorying your situation, but we're as smart as you are, and there's no getting out of this until we get what we want."

So he thinks.

I open both eyes to the blinding light, but I won't close them. I don't care how uncomfortable it is.

The guy I'd never seen before takes a step closer, still keeping me from seeing who is behind him and clearly the puppet master.

"Water," I croak.

"Not yet."

The person behind him moves, I can hear his footsteps approaching.

Guy in front asks, "Should I bag him?"

My breathing stays steady even though I'm anything but. That was the one weakness I had—being blind was the worst torture. I'd rather be beaten than have a fucking bag over my head.

"There's no need to," I say with my throat feeling as if it's on fire. "I don't know where I am anyway."

The orchestrator laughs, and I try to move to catch a glimpse, but all I see are camouflage pants and boots.

He's either military or got his hands on gear. If he were a SEAL, it would lend to Jackson's belief that the problems weren't stemming from his first wife's side. If I had it wrong . . .

It means that I could've been followed and that what I saw wasn't real.

What if this is a guy from Jackson's past military time?

It could be a SEAL or any number of options.

My mind is still a little slow, and it takes me a second to register the guy in front of me has stepped to the side and now has a gun pointed at my head.

I look over at the other guy, the one who is clearly in charge. Our eyes meet for just a second and I freeze in disbelief, not believing this could be true.

"Hey, buddy."

Then the bag is dropping over my head and a sound that no soldier can mistake rings out.

chapter thirty-seven

PAIN.

Pain like nothing I've ever known tears through my body. I scream out, wanting to stop it. Trying to wail against it. Praying for it to stop because surely this means I'm dying.

There is no way anyone can live through this.

The sounds of my screams echo around me.

All I register is blood as my body begins to shut down from the sheer agony . . .

So much blood.

And then I feel nothing.

to be continued . . .

books by
CORINNE MICHAELS

The Salvation Series

Beloved

Beholden

Consolation

Conviction

Defenseless

Evermore: A Salvation Series Novella

Indefinite

Infinite

Return to Me Series

Say You'll Stay

Say You Want Me

Say I'm Yours

Say You Won't Let Go: A Return to Me/Masters and Mercenaries Novella

Second Time Around Series

We Own Tonight

One Last Time

Not Until You

If I Only Knew

Co-Written Novels with Melanie Harlow

Hold You Close

Imperfect Match

acknowledgements

To my husband and children. You sacrifice so much for me to continue to live out my dream. Days and nights of me being absent even when I'm here. I'm working on it. I promise. I love you more than my own life.

My readers. There's no way I can thank you enough. It still blows me away that you read my words. You guys have become a part of my heart and soul.

Bloggers: I don't think you guys understand what you do for the book world. It's not a job you get paid for. It's something you love and you do because of that. Thank you from the bottom of my heart.

My beta reader Melissa Saneholtz: Dear God, I don't know how you still talk to me after all the hell I put you through. Your input and ability to understand my mind when even I don't blows me away. If it weren't for our phone calls, I can't imagine where this book would've been. Thank you for helping me untangle the web of my brain.

My assistant, Christy Peckham: How many times can one person be fired and keep coming back? I think we're running out of times. No, but for real, I couldn't imagine my life without you. You're a pain in my ass but it's because of you that I haven't fallen apart.

Sarah Hansen for once again making these covers perfect.

Melanie Harlow, thank you for being the good witch in our duo or Ethel to my Lucy. Your friendship means the world to me and I love writing with you. I feel so blessed to have you in my life.

Bait, Stabby, and Corinne Michaels Books—I love you more than you'll ever know.

My agent, Kimberly Brower, I am so happy to have you on my team. Thank you for your guidance and support.

Melissa Erickson, you're amazing. I love your face. Thank you for always talking me off the ledge that is mighty high.

To my narrators, Andi Arndt and Jason Clarke who bring these characters to life in a way that only you two can. Andi, your friendship over these last few years has only grown and I love your heart so much. Thank you for always having my back.

Vi, Claire, Mandi, Amy, Kristy, Penelope, Kyla, Rachel, Tijan, Alessandra, Meghan, Laurelin, Kristen, Devney, Jessica, Carrie Ann, Kennedy, Lauren, Susan, Sarina, Beth, Julia, and Natasha—Thank you for keeping me striving to be better and loving me unconditionally. There are no better sister authors than you all.

about the author

New York Times, USA Today, and *Wall Street Journal* Bestseller Corinne Michaels is the author of multiple bestselling novels. She's an emotional, witty, sarcastic, and fun-loving mom of two beautiful children. Corinne is happily married to the man of her dreams and is a former Navy wife.

After spending months away from her husband while he was deployed, reading and writing was her escape from the loneliness. She enjoys putting her characters through intense heartbreak and finding a way to heal them through their struggles. Her stories are chock full of emotion, humor, and unrelenting love.

CPSIA information can be obtained
at www.ICGtesting.com
Printed in the USA
FSHW021254260619
59454FS